To family and friends. May this serve as a reminder that the strongest chapters are born from the toughest times.

Edited by

Devika Sharma

THE MOVING TYPE

AUSTIN MACAULEY PUBLISHERS™
LONDON • CAMBRIDGE • NEW YORK • SHARJAH

Copyright © Devika Sharma 2021

The right of Devika Sharma to be identified as project coordinator author of this work has been asserted by the author in accordance with Federal Law No. (7) of UAE, Year 2002, Concerning Copyrights and Neighboring Rights.

All rights reserved. No part of this publication may be reproduced, stored in a retrieval system, or transmitted in any form or by any means, electronic, mechanical, photocopying, recording, or otherwise, without the prior permission of the publishers.

Any person who commits any unauthorized act in relation to this publication may be liable to legal prosecution and civil claims for damages.

The age group that matches the content of the books has been classified according to the age classification system issued by the National Media Council.

ISBN – 9789948831297 – (Paperback)

Printer Name: iPrint Global Ltd
Printer Address: Witchford, England

Application Number: MC-10-01-0193142
Age Classification: E

First Published 2021
AUSTIN MACAULEY PUBLISHERS FZE
Sharjah Publishing City
P.O Box [519201]
Sharjah, UAE
www.austinmacauley.ae
+971 655 95 202

To my parents for always overestimating my ability to write. To my brother for balancing the scales and keeping me humble. To Vish for believing in this idea more than I did. To Sam for answering every 4 am phone call; this book would have remained incomplete if it wasn't for you. To Azeen and Nishant for keeping me sane. To my aunty Astrid for hyping me up. To my publisher for taking on this crazy concept. And to every single one of the 121 authors and 8 illustrators; words aren't enough. Thank you for making this possible.

Thank you for moving with us.

— Devika Sharma
Creator of the Moving Type

1 Story
35 Chapters, 122 Writers

Chapter 1
By Devika Sharma

Illustrated by Neil Zuzarte

Four unhappy faces in squares across the laptop screen were forced to smile.

"Could you guys stay still and try to look a little happier?" urged Tara with her phone held up, ready to capture a moment in time no one wanted to be a part of. It was Day 6 of the lockdown and everyone was starting to feel it.

"At least we get to work in our pajamas," Adi offered.

Only if you still have a job, thought Rob as he picked up his controller to resume the new Street Fight IV game he had played nonstop over the last few days. As his character shot up a grocery store and rode away on a red Harley Davidson to the sound of police sirens, Rob spoke up for the first time during their group call, "Hey, did you guys manage to spot any of the drones flying around? That's how they're watching the streets."

Reflexively a few heads turned toward their nearest windows. There was a photo-like stillness outside. Uncomfortable with the quiet, Nadia tapped on her window along to the sound of smooth jazz that filled her bedroom. Hard to imagine the post-apocalyptic worlds that only existed in the movies had suddenly become their own. In a quick few months, the entire world had stopped fighting with each other and were forced to combat one common enemy. One that wasn't racist, sexist, or political; the relentless virus Budlyt-19, fittingly dubbed by the media as *The Seeker*. Scientists were saying a wet market hosted by poor hygienic conditions presented a unique opportunity that allowed the virus to make the jump from snakes to human beings. And the virus had spread. *Fast.* It had claimed over 15,000 lives in only three months, announcing its arrival with two deceptively common symptoms: fever and sweats. Three weeks later if you woke up to a bloody nose, it was already too late. As medical professionals scrambled for answers, the healthy charged to the nearest hospitals confusing the common cold with *The Seeker*, wasting precious time and resources that were critical to the infected. Consequently, governments across the globe started to impose strict lockdowns resulting in people hiding scared in their own homes.

"Nope," replied Tara as an intrusive flash went off. She thumbed through a couple of filters finally settling on one that adjusted the light so that her nose looked slimmer, and clicked 'Post.' Her phone lit up almost immediately to a steady stream of notifications.

Nadia eyed the picture and laughed. "You can see the mess in my room, thanks, T. This isn't how I want to appear to the masses." Last year a video of Tara doing her makeup using only cooking ingredients went fairly viral and now she was in spitting distance to being Finsta Famous. Rested against an expensive monochromatic art piece of the city's oldest tower, Tara wasn't listening. She seemed more distracted by her phone than usual.

The iconic Trida Tower was a short walk away from each of their houses and was home to a beautiful cinema that was recently refurbished and even boasted a highly acclaimed chef whose wholesome food and foul mouth made for an entertainment experience that saw everyone from hormonal tweens to erratic families to passive pensioners shuffle in and out of their giant golden revolving doors. The country of Matana was blessed with enough beauty but it was the brains behind the city that made it a contemporary hotspot for tourists all year round. With numbers doubling year on year, it eventually was the greed that resulted in Matana being one of the last to close its borders.

"The gravity of the situation is only starting to come to light," remarked their sweaty Prime Minister Greoff. Ironic choice of words considering the predictions for some very dark times ahead.

In an effort to salvage their sanity through solidarity, the four friends got on a call at least once a day to check-in and download on each other. Or as Adi liked to call it their *compos mentis*.

"Adi, what should we do about dinner?" quizzed Nadia. Her older cousin was the only relative she had in town so moving down the hall from him in an apartment complex smack in the middle of the city encouraged a big sigh of relief from their families back home. And, for a bachelor in his late twenties, Adi was a phenomenal cook.

"I think we could manage some pasta," replied Adi, "I'll check the kitchen."

He got up to leave and Rob yelled after him, "I can't wait to come over once this is over. I miss your lasagna, man."

A few minutes later after exhausting the customary sighs of frustration, exchanging holiday dreams in exotic locations and opinions on what shows were the most binge-worthy, Tara yawned and said her goodbyes. She had to call her parents and wanted to try out some quarantine themed video ideas before bed. Rob said he had a game with his brother and left the chat not long after. Adi still hadn't reappeared in his square.

A round of applause outside Nadia's window cut through the catchy riff of the song; it had become a tradition in the city for people to lean outside their windows and show their support towards everyone from the medical professionals to the delivery boys for a few minutes each night. It was now past 9 pm. As she slipped on her fluffy slides to make her way over to Adi's, a message popped up on her phone from a number she did not recognize. It simply read: "*Be careful of the door to the left of your floor.*"

Chapter 2
By Surabhi Choudhary

Illustrated by Mahesh Perera

Nadia froze. Her hand hovered over the hook on the wall where she usually hung the house keys. She went through the text message again. Could it be a prank? Maybe it was just some friend goofing around using a number she didn't know they had. The message itself was intriguing enough. But what made it outright eerie was the fact that it had been sent to her by a complete stranger. A loud whirring noise broke her reverie. She pulled the blinds away from the windowpane to see a surveillance drone flying over their neighborhood just like Rob had said. Looking down, she could spot a handful of soldiers milling around the crossroads that had been barricaded since the lockdown. They were checking all the vehicles passing through which, admittedly, weren't many. Even as Nadia continued to watch, a driver was escorted to a van emblazoned with the insignia of the Republic of Matana Armed Forces stationed near the curb to get his credentials verified. Life, as she knew it, had changed so drastically since the pandemic. She sighed. She was overthinking again.

She had to talk to someone about the odd message. Praying she hadn't gone to bed yet, Nadia swiftly dialed Tara's number and waited for her to answer her phone. Her heart sank deeper with every bell that went unanswered until the line got disconnected. She didn't want her parents to get worried when the times were troubled already. Who else could she talk to? *Adi*, a voice said in her head. Her cousin was a very kind person and Nadia knew he would patiently hear her out and not make fun of her later, in case the message turned out to be a silly prank. The burden pressing her down ever since she'd received the text message seemed to be lightening a little already. Yes, she could talk to him.

Stepping out of her apartment, Nadia couldn't help but look out of the corner of her eye at the only door to the left of the floor that she and Adi lived on. It stood in semi-darkness at the end of the dimly lit corridor. Just looking at it sent a shiver down her spine. Closing her eyes, she turned around and began making her way to Adi's apartment at the other end of the hallway. She couldn't help but feel she was being watched until she reached his place.

"There you are! I thought you'd ditched me and my Arrabiata," Adi answered the door with a broad smile on his face. His brightly lit drawing-room immediately made her feel better.

Nadia gave her cousin a watery smile as she sank into a sofa. With his intelligent eyes behind the rimless glasses, chiseled jawline and curly hair, Adi could easily pass off as a model. Except that he wasn't. He was one of the most promising young scientists at LifaLabs, Matana's biggest pharmaceutical company. A brilliant pharmacologist whose job was to create and test new drugs, Adi was on the HealPlus team that was trying to find a remedy for Budlyt-19. This meant that most of his days were spent in the laboratory and he was buried under his books, journals, and laptop whenever he could get a chance to come back home for a few hours. Feeling calmer, Nadia decided that the story could wait until they'd had dinner.

They did the dishes after polishing off the excellent pasta and moved back to the sitting area when Nadia decided to broach the topic. However, Adi spoke up before she could even open her mouth.

"We've initiated human trials for the vaccine against Budlyt-19," he said opening a bottle of wine, oblivious to her discomfort. Downing her drink in 2–3 gulps, she couldn't hold it in any longer.

"Adi, I got a text today. I'm scared," she blurted out the entire story.

To her utter disbelief, she saw his expressions shift for a moment. There was a knowing gleam in his eyes that vanished almost as soon as it'd appeared. He cleared his throat and forced a laugh.

"It has to be a prankster, Nadia. Do you want more wine?" he changed the topic abruptly, raising her suspicions.

She shook her head and thanked him for the dinner.

"Forget that it happened. Okay?" his words echoed in the silent corridor as she left.

Adi knew something that he wasn't ready to admit. She couldn't shake off the feeling that she'd actually sunk further in the quicksand. Nadia felt confused and lightheaded as she reached her apartment. As if being drawn by a magnet, she felt an urge to find out what was hidden beyond the sinister door. She began walking to the end of the corridor, the sound of her footsteps bouncing off the dark, peeling walls. The lone, flickering light cast long shadows that seemed to move. Nadia wiped the sweat beads on her forehead as she approached the door. Was it the deathly silence playing tricks on her ears or was there a harsh, guttural groaning emanating from beyond? She swallowed a couple of times, wiped her sweaty palms on her shorts, and reached for the doorknob.

"I told you to forget about this door," whispered a voice into her ear.

Nadia jumped out of her skin, screaming out of fright and dropped her phone. Her heart thumping wildly, she turned around to find Adi who had snuck up behind her noiselessly.

"You know what's in there?" she croaked.

Adi nodded and fished out a key from his pocket.

"And since you're so nosy about this, let me show you," he said offhandedly.

As the door creakily swung open, a scene so macabre greeted Nadia that she fainted.

Adi reached down and pocketed her phone. Then he dialed a number, surveying the gruesome room.

"Yes?" a voice answered in hushed tones.

"We have a situation here," Adi said, staring at Nadia.

Chapter 3
By Julia Malone

Co-authors: Dipanwita Du, Laura Chamberland, Darwin Battaglia, Amy Lentini

Illustrated by Lennita D'Coutho

Tara checked her phone, wondering why Nadia hadn't joined the call. She'd been listening to Rob and Adi drone on for a while. As much as she enjoyed these calls with her friends, something about their daily catch-ups made her realize how desperately bleak their lives had become in lockdown. That was the stark reality of their situation. Everyone knew it.

"How am I supposed to get a job in isolation," Rob asked in answer to Adi's query. "Not everyone can be working on the budvirus."

"Budlyt-19... Lots of people are working from home. Online companies or whatever must be hiring. Monopolize on all of this, you know?" Adi said.

Rob shrugged. Blond hair fell into his face as he turned back to the television where he was playing yet another Street Fight game against his brother. Netflix and video games were the only entertainment during this hard time. Life was locked to the virtual screen, cutting off the real world. That, and the endless hours one can spend in the kitchen, baking yet another bread. Adi bent over his book again.

Tara sighed, looking back at her phone. Twenty minutes and Nadia still hadn't joined them. Nadia was never more than two minutes late to these calls, it was so unlike her. Tara had sent five texts, all of which went unanswered. Five. Nadia, responsive and organized, would never ignore her messages.

Tara's hand hovered over her emails once more. Constantly checking her phone had become almost a compulsion during the early days of the pandemic, and now... Tapping the side of her phone with a thumb, she thought. The anonymous email had been bothering her all day. Just as soon as something interesting had happened, after months of boredom, she wished desperately that it hadn't. She tore her eyes away from the bright screen and looked back at the tiny squares of her friends.

"Where's Nadia?" Tara asked.

Rob and Adi, both absorbed in their respective hobbies, ignored her.

"Adi? Adi!"

Adi must know.

"Adi!"

Adi started. He looked back at her, pushing his glasses further up the bridge of his crooked nose. It was the one flaw in his model-like appearance and yet, Tara mused, it somehow made him even more appealing.

"Sorry?" he said.

"Where's Nadia?"

"Oh." He fixed his glasses again, taking the time to run a hand through his curly hair. "She's busy...with work," he replied with an indecisive voice.

"Work?" Tara's brow creased. "Is she performing on a live-stream? I'll check it out." She reached for her phone. Maybe Nadia would be joining the masses of artists trending on the social waves.

"Right." Adi scratched his chin. "Not work. She's talking to her parents."

"They call every morning at eight. That was ages ago."

Was Adi acting odd? Elusive?

"Is something wrong?"

Adi's eyes shuttered. Social cues may be harder to decipher on endless zoom calls, but even on the screen, she could see a shift in his demeanor.

Tara attempted to speak again but Adi rose, cutting her off.

"I'll go get her."

He sauntered away. Tara heard the slam of his apartment door and was left staring at the leather couch.

"Is he acting strange?" Tara asked Rob.

Rob grunted, pressing several buttons on his controller before looking at her.

"Dunno," he shrugged. "Adi's busy." Rob resumed his game and she heard the revving of an engine. Adi's apartment door slammed again. His screen was covered by the bulk of two figures as they squeezed onto the couch. Tara quickly turned up the volume on her laptop, trying to hear what Adi was saying under his breath but the audio kept cutting in and out. The tone was strange, almost forceful, but she couldn't catch the mumbled words before the audio jumped back to Rob's game.

Nadia now sat to Adi's left. Coils of curly brown hair fell messily across her shoulders. Was she paler today? It was difficult to tell with the harsh lighting.

"Nadia," Tara said, "what took you so long?"

Tara waited for an answer, a beat more than was normal, she thought.

Nadia stared blankly at the screen and then, as Adi gently touched her elbow, she blinked.

"I was speaking with my mom," she said, voice clipped. "She called again."

Rob looked up and Tara could see from the slight frown on his face that he too had heard something off in her voice.

"You okay?" Tara asked.

Nadia blinked, rapidly. "Yes."

"Look, guys," Adi interrupted, "we better go. Nadia left the oven on." He rested a hand on her shoulder. "We don't want to burn down the complex." Adi smiled.

"Yes…" Nadia said, following Adi's quavering tone. "Oh dear. I did." Her voice was slow, as if she had fallen into a trance.

"We'll talk tomorrow," Adi said. He waved.

"Okay. But—"

Adi ended his video. Tara stared solely at Rob now.

That was all wrong, she thought.

Tara bit her lip, looking down at her phone. Nadia's pale skin. Her glassy eyes. Tara thought back to the video attachment she'd received that afternoon. An anonymous message had been sent to her, signed off simply by *A Follower.* She'd passed it off as a hoax, hadn't really paid attention. But now…

Her phone buzzed. Tara's eyes widened. *A Follower* had sent another message. She clicked on the attachment. Nadia stared back at her. Only it wasn't Nadia.

"What the—" Tara spoke aloud, realizing it only a moment later when Rob's head shot up from his game.

"What?"

Could she share this with him? Because this was something she couldn't handle on her own – if it was true. But Rob was close with Adi and Adi was definitely acting odd, Tara thought. She looked back at Rob who was watching her expectantly, the most interested he'd appeared in days.

"Nothing," Tara said. "I've got to go."

She shut off her video, fingers trembling. Clutching her phone in one hand, she took a second to steady herself. No matter what danger she was about to get herself into, she had to be strong for her friend. Tara put on a jacket, grabbed her car keys, and locked the door behind her.

Chapter 4
By Rebecca Steel

Co-authors: Parul Mehta, James Maybon, Angela Maybon, Sarah Saeed, Nayab Hussain

Illustrated by Bhoomi Satwani

Since leaving the apartment, Adi had resumed taking control of Nadia, gripping firmly onto her forearm. "You almost blew that one, cus, bad move." He pushed her along in haste, heading in the direction of the apartment to the left of Nadia's. The irony, she thought, that the message which intended to warn her had led her directly toward horrors behind that very door.

A glow shone under the door frame; someone was inside. Adi unlocked the door, poked his head around the doorway, and began surveying the room.

"Ken, it's you, okay good," he dragged Nadia inside and threw her to the ground. "Someone tipped Nadia off about the apartment. I thought I would try and get her off our case by showing her the room, but someone had already begun moving people inside. I hate saying it, as she is my cousin, but we have to do something. She saw some of the subjects' bodies."

Nadia wanted to believe she heard a twinge in his voice, but the reality of the situation was she no longer recognized the cold and calculating man that stood before her. She could just stare at him, willing him to look at her, hoping to see his eyes crinkle as he laughed, pulling her off the floor and showing off some industry grade human body replicas. But his eyes didn't crinkle.

And, there was no avoiding the smell...oh the smell of something rotten. And dead.

The conversation they had just had in his apartment came reverberating through the fog in her head. *Human trials.*

Ken squinted his eyes and stared at Adi for a good minute before responding, "You're an idiot Adi; it looks like you have already drugged the girl, what do you want me to do with her; add her to the experiment, kill her... I dunno, you tell me, man."

Adi knew he had to make a decision but damn, who knew it was going to get this complicated. Adi put his head down and murmured, "Add her to the experiment." He took one last look at Nadia, shook his head, and walked in the direction of the front door. Just as he reached for the handle, he heard a familiar voice calling out in the hallway. "Nadia, just open the door, we need to talk. It is me, Nadia, It's Tara. Nadia you're scaring me, answer the damn door."

Adi paused, turned his head toward Ken and suggested that he come to the door. "Shit. This chick is persistent. She is Nadia's best friend, and she knows something is up. I don't think I'm going to be able to get rid of her that easily." Adi put his hands to his head and assumed a stress pose. "The last thing we want is to have the cops called or bloody drones circling in on this area."

Ken didn't need to say anything. He knew he was grabbing both girls. He walked back toward his briefcase, pulled out a syringe and a vial of an unlabeled liquid. He drew up 10 ml of the liquid, walked straight up to the door, eased Adi to his left, propped open the door and began walking calmly up to Tara.

"Hi there, I'm Ken, you looking for Nadia?" Tara paused and stared at the tall, muscular man; a million thoughts began running through her head. Mainly, *How the hell does this guy know Nadia?! I've never seen this guy before.*

Tara replied, "Yeah, you seen her?"

Ken pointed toward the door to the left. "She is in there; you're welcome to head on in."

Tara's spidey senses began kicking in, and she knew something was very wrong here. No way was she entering some random dude's apartment. She would swing by with

Rob later. With a slight quiver in her voice, she responded to Ken, "Um, nah it's okay. She can call me when she's done. I've um… I've left something in the oven. I better go… But uh, thanks."

Tara turned to walk away. In the corner of her eye, she caught a glimpse of Ken's arm reaching out toward her. On instinct her body jerked forward to avoid him. As she began to run, Ken stabbed the needle into her arm with his left hand and began pulling her to a halt with his right. The room began to spin. Tara fell to the ground.

Ken scooped Tara up, looked around to make sure no one had seen them and calmly carried her back to the apartment. Ken lay Tara on the couch, turned to Adi and said, "For a smart guy, you are the biggest screw up I know. You better get your shit together before word spreads to the boss."

It was better not to get into it with Ken while he was on the backfoot. Adi acknowledged Ken with a nod of the head, took another look at Nadia laying in the corner of the room, and then proceeded to leave the apartment. Adi pulled his phone from his pocket and began dialing 555-974-6787.

Chapter 5
By Matt Fudge

Illustrated by Mahesh Perera

His phone, still sticky, buzzed. The sides were marked with the faint, crusting smears of chocolate, one of the few vices he had left. Rob groped around for the phone, knocking an ashtray half-off the coffee table so that it teetered over the edge. He wouldn't notice until later when he would knock it off completely. He picked up the phone, scrolling his notifications, (such as they were) with a sort of determined detachment. MyFitt wanted him to "FIND HIS FIT TODAY!" His grandma had called – well, good for her, she was figuring out the new phone. Jules (Or was it Julia? Julianna?) had snapped him; ahh, he hardly knew her anyways, and if he wasn't gonna get laid, she wasn't worth the effort. And... Nothing from Nadia.

He thought back to a few days before quarantine started. It felt like thinking way back, like thinking back into middle school or the summer of '15. A few weeks ago, he'd been riding high – figuratively and literally. Nadia. *That girl...* She was one of those, and he knew it. He shook his head and laughed at himself, disparagingly, and thought back to '15 after all. He'd never change, not in five years, not in a hundred. She wasn't the first of those girls, and God knows, she wouldn't be the last; but she was one of them. One of the ones that hit like a light post at 120 kph: which is to say, he wrapped his head around them. Couldn't let go of them. He laughed again and tried – and failed – to roll off the couch. But he'd been making advances. The wheels had been turning, the engine had been running, the river had been flowing. In the first two and a half years of their acquaintance, he'd been an extra, he felt, in the grand epic that was the life of Nadia, the one, the only. But now? Well okay, he'd been playing a supporting lead at the very least. That had been weeks ago. Worse, he'd gotten off on a heavy load to celebrate – he'd been so high, he'd thought Adi had been kicking around in his apartment, how loaded was that? – a heavy load that had made itself known, fivefold, when the lockdown hit for real. After that, he'd have killed for any kind of score. Hell, even the cough syrup he'd picked up with his groceries (if you could indeed call them "groceries") had seemed like a wild ride the night before. A sort of schoolyard high, but it hadn't even worn off yet, and he was a little slow-moving this morning, to say the least. Maybe that's why he didn't feel it – the beginning of something, something he was gonna be afraid of. Not yet, no. But soon.

Was it morning? He lost track of the hours wondering about Nadia. Had he said something wrong? Probably. Maybe she was dead. That cracked him up all over again. More likely that Adi guy had called her off it; heard them on the phone or something and talked her out of it. Yeah, it happened. That bio guy, what a type. He could make a hell of a lasagna though, that was true. Rob got up. Easier said than done, with the last of the 150-odd milligrams still swimming around in his veins, but he did it. Maybe he'd get himself an omelet. Yeah, chop up some greens, pour some milk, turn this thing around. Do some push-ups. Read a book. Man, today was full of laughs. She'd been on the call the other day, that much was true. For once, he'd been glad he was so sober; he was used to hanging out with those guys on his own terms when he was expecting it. They were good company, those three, even before he'd staked out Nadia as his kind of girl. That sounded so predatory, goddamn. He wasn't that bad – even before he'd noticed Nadia as something more than a friend. But he never really had them over. He'd always have to stow all the ashtrays, like a damn flight attendant. Half the time he felt as if he was wearing one of their little collars too. They were adults, but somehow, it wouldn't feel right sitting around and burning some hay with them. If they didn't report him or something.

He got another chocolate bar and sat down again, this time, in his armchair. "Indubitably," he muttered, feeling like his old man. The phone went off again. An email. An email? It was anonymous, carrying all that air of vague professionalism that emails implied to him. Had he applied for a job he forgot? This was a new email, he doubted he'd have too many fliers coming in yet. As it turned out, it wasn't a flier, nor an add. Well, he thought it was, but he didn't have a choice to buy, not really. Quite the opposite. He'd been bought, in a sense. Bought, and he didn't even know it. Did he? Was there a new heaviness in his already leaden arms? Were his eyes just a bit drier? Did he slump down, even just a bit further? Maybe. Maybe he did. But he thought it was just an add. "We want YOU! Support your nation! Beta tests running now – sign up to earn a moderate paycheck and do your part against the virus!" It was blocked, in bold, over a stock image of a smiling doctor. This was the kind of thing Adi would be running, that he was sure of. Should he sign up? Ah, what the hell, cash was cash. Maybe he would. For now, he figured he'd finally work up the courage to call her… Had he said something wrong? Tara could tell him. Yeah, he'd call her first. Okay. Okay. Call one, get the other. Call one, call the next, tell her all about it…and in a week or two, it's you and Nadia, right here in this chair, how about that? Indubitably, yeah, that could work. He dialed her up, and wondered if he ever would change. Nah. It may as well be '15.

Chapter 6
By Daisy Ballard

Illustrated by Lennita D'Coutho

Tara tried to lift her woozy head but it was as heavy as iron, her limbs felt like they were slowly being dipped in molten lava; the pain was excruciating. Through the haze of drugs something registered in her brain, she was tied up. The dizziness and pain seemed to dissipate for a moment as her general horror condensed into the pure fear of being confined. She struggled against the ropes for a second before the torment to her limbs came back and she could hardly bring herself to twitch a finger. Closing her eyes, Tara strained her mind back to the vague recollection she had before her blackout. It was tough, her thoughts were sluggish. All she remembered was the stab of a needlepoint in her arm and some guy. What was his name? Kim? Kevin? Ugh she didn't know. There was someone else there too. She was sure of that. But her mind was sinking, losing its grasp on the present already. Then there was someone's face, it swam into view right before her eyes. *Adi!* Tara let out a groan – all her body would allow and a final thought before she sank back into unconsciousness. How could her friend do this to her?

A few hours later, Tara opened her eyes again. She felt strangely light, like a ten-ton weight had been lifted off her. The ropes had seemingly vanished and her thoughts were as clear as the sea in the Mediterranean where she'd once been on holiday. Aside from the burns that the ropes had left, the pain in her arms had gone and in fact, if it had not been for the stark, white lighting and the uncomfortable cold of the metal table she was sitting on, she might've thought it had all been a dream. But she knew better. Tara had still not forgotten feeling like she was literally made of fire. It was kind of hard to forget. What was harder was knowing her best friend was stuck inside with those two men. Tara's thoughts wandered to Nadia for a moment. They'd been best friends since high school but lately she felt like something different was happening between them, at least at Tara's end anyways. It was just – every time she looked her in the eye, something stirred in Tara's gut that she couldn't quite explain. She had to get Nadia out of there. The door was locked – of course, but Tara couldn't give up at the smallest hurdle. There was no denying that she was smart. With her straight blonde hair and startling blue eyes, she fooled everyone into thinking she was a walking 'dumb blonde' stereotype but anyone who bothered to get to know her knew otherwise. A million ideas began running through her head, each more unconvincing than the last. If she was strong she could break the door down, or attack someone if they came through the door. But she'd never seen the point in acquiring any physical strength, let alone learning to throw a punch, besides it might be days before someone came through the door and by then Adi would've had the time to seriously injure Nadia.

Desperately Tara looked around the room for something that might be able to help her escape. Her eyes landed on the fire extinguisher. *That could work,* she thought to herself. Pulling it from the wall, she raised it above her head, poised to smash down that damn door. With all the strength that she could muster, Tara rammed the fire extinguisher against the door, it rattled but didn't budge. Arms sore from holding it above her head, Tara leaned against the wall, breathing heavily and braced herself to do it again. The second time the wood splintered and the door slammed open with an almighty crash! Not wasting any time, Tara ran out of what appeared to be a storage room and quickly realized she was still in Nadia's apartment block. But that meant... *Adi!* Adrenaline kicked in and Tara made a break for the stairs. As she reached the door to the stairwell, she heard his familiar voice shout out behind her. How had she never seen this dark side of him before? She'd always thought of him as gentle, he wouldn't even kill the spiders that appeared in his apartment.

Tara made it out onto the main road, wishing that the streets were full of people, like they used to be before lockdown. Then she would've had a chance by slipping into the crowd. Fast-paced footsteps behind her told Tara that Adi hadn't given up, he was chasing her but she couldn't get caught, not after being this close to getting away. Tara ran until the stitch needling itself into her side got so painful she collapsed on the floor, her back slumped against an old phone box. Tears were running down her face, she was exhausted, frightened, and worst of all…completely alone, without the comfort of home. Unable to go back with Adi looking for her. And what about Nadia? Was she all right? Had Adi hurt her? Suddenly, out of the silence came a ringing sound. It was the old phone box. That was weird, Tara thought, nobody used them anymore. Curiosity won over her trepidation and she went inside, answering the phone. A stranger's gravelly voice on the other end simply said, "Tara, listen, forget social distancing and the virus, there's more to this than you think. I can save your friend Nadia if you meet me in Byde park at 7:30 tomorrow. This isn't a prank, you're in real danger," before hanging up, leaving Tara to contemplate whether she should go or not with the stillness of the night.

Chapter 7
By Cal Castille

Illustrated by Neil Zuzarte

It didn't really matter that Tara had figured something out; she could be dealt with.

Adi wasn't dragged, powerless and naive, into it, despite what he'd later say. Instead of admitting, he'd claim that with coercion, threats, and bribery that capitalized on his vulnerability and poisoned him with persistence, he was manipulated to set up the apartment, to add that extra lock, to cut an extra key. Limited was his culpability if he was just an accessory to the 'scheme' as they called it – an ironic nod to film and a sincere shove in the direction of this idea being misanthropic at its core. Accessories, after all, were just support structures and held no real creative power or guilt, so it was useful that he could pretend to be one and let Ken seem like the leader when he needed to. In truth, the apartment was infested with pages of documents he'd written that shone with flowcharts of considered circumstances, possibilities, outcomes for their plan, and ways to spin each of them for positive public relations. One of his first realizations after the initial goal for what had now begun – that thing that would mutate to subvert everything else in his life – was that perception was everything.

Thuds and steps blasted and faded, dunking his head in cold water and indicating Tara's escape. He called after her. Ran after her. But he couldn't abandon his post for long and returned to the apartment without her. The phone purred rings, seemingly unsuccessful for the third time. '555-974-6787' stared back, unblinking, at him from the screen.

He sighed.

People, he thought, *are naive and impressionable and undeserving of autonomy, of progression.*

And from this opinion, this itch grew a condition so severe it enveloped him and colored his perspective toward humanity with shades of black and grey and red. The need to nurture this idea, to furnish his mind and the apartment with propaganda for it, became inescapable, and it was these attributes of our collective personality: the pastimes we enjoyed and the responsibilities we maintained and the rules we conformed to, that became the true accessories, not him.

Adi had spent years cultivating a persona and layering himself to appear mildly attractive and only just enticing enough to evoke a smile, never an action; it had all led to tonight and them, those idiots – well, just one idiot now, he thought – locked in what should still be his pure office, studio, resort. They had, through their misplaced curiosity, tainted it too early.

The skills to sustain this clean image were picked up easily; learning to cook and to be a dutiful family member was simple because it strengthened the cloak he wore, enabling the apartment to flourish so his revolution, as he privately called it, could keep growing to its bloom. No, it wasn't these palpable prisms he was seen through that were difficult, it was the pain of continuing to contribute to this false meritocracy that burned around him, flames rising the longer it took to bring it all crashing down. To stand together with society and collectively be this curtain, block the sordid truth behind it when he had the knowledge and the power to watch it open and fall, shatter and disintegrate, that was the hardest part. He longed to shuffle his feet in the ashes of its decay and whistle with delight, just like he did that night having dropped his facade with the opening of the apartment door. It provided him with warmth to be open and true to others apart from Ken; it felt like a step closer to going live and receiving the praise he would inevitably be washed with soon. Letting his mind wander amid the whining of Nadia who was already beginning to lose the blood from her face and to shrivel, ever so slightly, he imagined her within that delightful meadow of ash, of those ungrateful and therefore left behind. It would all be worth it.

Afterward, he would commission his first commemorative statue to be in the capital, in the center of the park. That seemed fitting, he realized.

What they, he, had built here would be the subject of dramatizations and museum exhibits for generations, he thought, be taught as a catalyst to human progress and be an epitome of the mantra that pain is temporary, victory is forever. Not that the pain would be his, or Ken's. No, they would be immune as the architects of change and as couriers to utopia; it was the passengers and the contrarians, people without foresight or initiative or grit, that would pay the price and burn for their better, more evolved, counterparts. Like Nadia, for example, and now, involved because of some misplaced loyalty or hamartia, like Tara too.

Just then, a voice, tinny and distant but authoritative, penetrating – sonar through the abyss – spoke. His benefactor had answered and now repeated, dragging Adi back from his mind, "What now?"

Chapter 8
By Mira Shah

Co-authors: Kshitij Mishra, Rocky D'Souza, Avneesh Mishra, Kini Mishra, Hasit Shah

Illustrated by Nishant Mishra

Hither and thither it all lay, Adi's growing apprehension, Nadia's tribulation, Rob's simplicity, and a stranger's call.

Tara's thoughts were in complete disarray at this point. The pang had subsided but left her with doubt. Doubt in herself, to why this transpired and why now? Why? She had invited that question many times with the choices she made in her life along with her inability to understand her friend's deeply rooted predicaments. It seemed like she had it all, yet she had none of it.

"If we believe in nothing, if nothing has any meaning and if we can affirm no values whatsoever, then everything is possible and nothing has any importance" – Camus' words tugged at her heart, as she looked at the nightscape drowsily through the cloudy glass.

A knock on the phone box, she turned to find Adi standing tall with a syringe in his hand, knocking still, smiling meekly. She was jolted awake by a security guard noisily knocking his baton against a residential gate across the street as dawn was starting to break. Used to waking up to the bustle of noise, the smell of freshly ground coffee, and to those that strode off to work with the promise of a new tomorrow, this new norm of silence was deafening.

Despite her bleak outlook on life, she found a purpose to finally do right, a selfish motive perhaps. Her thoughts unclouded, she knew what she had to do next as she ran. A few blocks ahead Tara stopped only for a few minutes outside a closed vintage record store. She loved that store. The records had kept her company during her teens and been her cheerleader when she needed it most. Like now. Tara tried to wipe away some of the dirt off her face but the grime and tears had left tracks down her cheeks that seemed to worsen with each swipe. She hardened her resolve and continued running.

Rob woke up disoriented to the sound of his phone. It was 6:55 am, a bit too early from his usual. He checked his phone to see if either Nadia or Tara had called before trying to go back to sleep. It was a bit strange that he hadn't heard from Tara, *she's always online*, he thought. A gentle chime cut through his thoughts. It wasn't his phone. The doorbell was ringing. Rob hesitantly dragged himself out of bed, tripping on the ashtray that powdered his carpet gray. As Rob slowly unlocked the door, Tara barged in and walked uninterruptedly toward the jug of water. She grabbed the blue and red checkered plastic by both hands and guzzled until the last drops fell all over her face and down her shirt.

"Those 10 missed calls from last night isn't a beacon call to show up unannounced at my house," said Rob. Tara glared at him, trying to catch her breath after chugging the water dry.

"I need your help," Tara said.

"It's an urgent Finsta photoshoot you want my help with, isn't it?" Rob mocked as he picked up a hairbrush and combed his hair while exaggerating his blinking, "Hey guys! It's me! Today we're going to discuss how to match our nails to our."

"Shut up, Rob! This is serious," she said. She sighed, wondering if she had made the right decision to seek help from this ex-jock who dissipated his time amusing himself by getting inebriated.

"Okay, this is going to sound unbelievable, so I need you to take a minute to process this before you laugh your head off."

She told him word for word what had happened in the past 12 hours, anticipating peals of laughter. The silence was deafening.

It felt like a lifetime had passed as Rob mutely continued to stare at her in the most peculiar way. Tara was beginning to get frustrated. Time was ticking away.

She glanced at the watch and continued, "Oh, and he said to meet him in Byde Park in 15 minutes as a matter of fact. I know this sounds crazy but…"

Rob gave her a long hard look before grabbing her hand and walking urgently toward the door. "There's no time. Let's discuss the plan on the way," he said.

Before Tara could get another word out, Rob interrupted as if he'd read her mind, "It isn't that hard to believe. I've known Adi for a while now and always felt something almost sinister about that perfect boy image." Rob caught himself. *Have I always felt this way or am I so jealous of Adi that I almost want this sick perversion to be true? Whatever it is, I should keep my feelings to myself for now. For all I know this could end up being one of those hidden camera pranks Tara is trying to pull off for content.*

"Okay then, I'll get right to it." said Tara, "I will be the one to communicate with the stranger and in no way are you to interrupt unless I've been compromised."

"So basically, you want me to be the hitman?"

"No, you goon! I'm not sure how he would react if he knew there were two of us since he only called me. Besides, we still don't know his motive behind all this. We need to be one step ahead of him," said Tara, "and I need your help watching out for the drones."

The conversation dampened when one thought crept into their minds. A real danger lay ahead of them, paranoia from the aftermath was certain. The past, present, and future interconnected and time slowly started to wear her down with despair. *Running in this readied state*, thought Tara, *nothing is more vexing than knowing there could be no tomorrow.*

They caught their breath at the gated entrance of the park while their eyes scanned the skies. "All clear," mouthed Rob, and Tara flashed him a thumbs up in return. They stealthily made their way inside. A little further ahead, they could see the silhouette of a man sitting on the park bench. His fire red hair appeared to burn in the sun. As expected, the park was empty and filled with white noise from the fauna hidden amidst the shades of green.

Rob gestured to Tara to go ahead and hid behind a tree. Tara could feel a lump in her throat as she daintily walked toward the stranger. Right then, Rob received a message notification. Tara turned around immediately, signaling Rob to turn off his phone. Rob's eyes widened as he read Adi's message.

Fear seized his bloodshot eyes as he looked up at Tara and dryly mouthed the words, "Run!"

Chapter 9
By Vishnu Sunil

Co-authors: Rachel Rajan, Conor Moran, Ginny George, Shawn Christopher, Lennox D'Coutho

Illustrated by Mahesh Perera

Panting, both Rob and Tara dropped down on the stain-ridden couch with a thud. Wanting to talk but barely being able to catch their breath, they just stared at each other hoping their eyes could communicate instead. They could hear their heartbeat After a few moments of getting their breath back,

Tara blurted out, "What happened? Why did we just run all the way back?"

Rob, still in a haze, partly from his splurge last night, replied, "I think Adi knows," and proceeded to show Tara the message which read *Why would you do this?*.

Tara's mouth fell as she grabbed the phone and reread the message over and over. She seemed to resemble one of those clowns at their local fair with their big mouths that you threw a ball into to win a goldfish or a ridiculously big stuffed toy. Her face remained frozen in horror and then jerked into a mini panic attack as Rob's phone started to ring with the face of her former captive, it was Adi calling and both of them looked at each other wondering what to do next.

"Umm, hey Adi," said Rob groggily trying to sound like the last hour or so was all just a bad dream.

"Bro, why are you doing this? You know you should have come to me first! I would have sorted this fix for you. What do you have to say for yourself??" quizzed Adi leaving the two friends sinking into the couch. "Just don't make me look bad in front of pharmacists whom I deal with, can't be seen being friends with a junkie. That would mess up my reputation, man," a sense of relief took over their shoulders that finally unclenched. "No one needs five bottles of cough syrup a week."

"I'm sorry Adi, I didn't tell the gang yet but I've lost my job and I'm going down this dark hole. The only option I can see right now is to enroll in this random beta drug test or something they're running. I need to be able to pay my rent, let alone survive or I'd rather this virus get me."

A moment of silence followed, Tara glaring at Rob for keeping a secret, Rob shying away and a silence of deliberation from Adi who was obviously contemplating something.

"I think I could help you with that," muttered Adi, "I know the Head Scientist running the tests and I could get you in but as long as you don't have any drugs in your system, so come clean to me now!"

"Clean as a whistle, except for maybe some excessive amounts of over-the-counter cough syrup," weirdly chuckled Rob.

Adi after quick deliberation agreed, "Hold on tight, I'll get back to you once I confirm with Dr. Rosenberg," and cut off.

Rob, still embarrassed to show his face to Tara, sat quietly, the consequences of the previous night starting to take effect. Tara started her rant with how Rob couldn't confide in his clique and then onto his new addiction, sounding more like a stressed mother than friend.

Words like "reckless" and "stupid" dominated most of her sentences. *Ironic,* thought Rob. But now wasn't the time to point any fingers.

Their relationship dynamic always perplexed him. Sometimes it was impossible to believe that the two of them could be friends but somehow, here they were, Tara still yelling at him.

"Are you done now? Thank you, Mom," scoffed Rob. "Do you think he's onto us? Is this a ruse to drug me up like he did you?"

Tara looked confused and stressed, her exhaustion from the escape catching up to her, "I'm not sure, maybe he's just being a good friend? Maybe he thinks he's smarter than everyone else that he's playing along with his God complex?" wrinkles more pronounced starting to appear on her forehead, *a look that would cause all my Finsta followers to immediately unfollow me*, she thought.

Was she that shallow? Is that what her mind had drifted to? Shoo away her friend for slaughter, act like nothing had happened, and go back to providing her followers with their daily dose of Taraness.

"We need to figure out what we're supposed to do. What about that guy? Do you know how to get in touch with this creepy stranger who called you?" quizzed Rob, starting to feel his heartbeat pulsing.

Tara on the verge of tears, "I don't know, about the guy, or about Nadia," her name finally got Tara to shed tears.

Not knowing what else he could do, he wrapped her around his monolithic arms, "We'll figure this out, let's just breathe, calm down, and figure out how we can go about this. Adi has got connections everywhere in the government, we need to be smart about this."

He continued to awkwardly pat her back as she grew smaller and smaller in his arms. As much as he wanted to help, his emotional stuntedness had rendered him useless in the face of tears. His eyes reflexively scanned the room for a bottle.

The ring of a message cut across the tension, it was Adi. *Meet me at my apartment tonight; I got you into the trial. Clean yourself up, I'll make you some lasagna like you wanted before we get started. I'll send a car for you at 6.* A message which wasn't as panic-inducing as the last.

Rob recited the text to Tara who had her fingers pressed to her temples. "It's okay. That's fine. We can figure it out," she chanted under her breath. She got up and began to pace the length of the room. Adi's message gave them a few hours to plan and a few more much needed hours for Rob to recuperate and prepare.

Chapter 10
By Azmeen Wadia

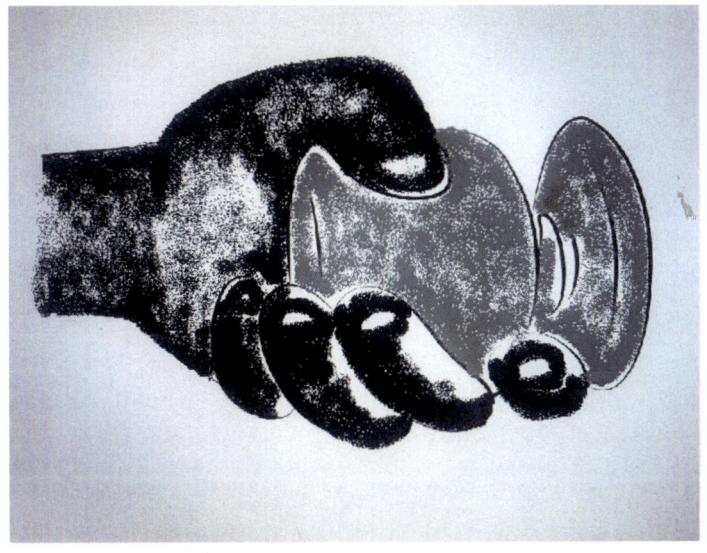

Illustrated by Bhoomi Satwani

The virus had been menacing Matana for months and finding a vaccine was the only hope left.

Rob's pickup arrived on the dot. He was both anxious and excited about the trial. Meanwhile, Tara was still pacing. She felt lost without her cell phone, but for now, Rob's computer sufficed as the only means she had to communicate with the outside world. Besides, Tara hadn't heard from her 'secret messenger,' although she had no doubt that sooner or later he would try to reach her again.

As Rob entered the apartment, his senses were engulfed by the stench of medical paraphernalia. Adi skittered across to Rob, pulled him into a makeshift area, and ticked off a list of requirements for every participant. Breathing check. Vitals check.

"Okay, Rob, we good," quipped Adi. Rob was handed out a somber-looking garment, like the ones worn in hospitals. He reluctantly slipped into his hideous Johnny gown. He was seated in the waiting area along with two nervous-looking individuals. A blonde woman, who appeared pretty sullen, and a man in his late fifties. He stretched his hand out to introduce himself, "Hey, I'm Rob." The woman ignored his advances, while the old man reciprocated with a firm handshake. "Samuel...Sam is fine..."

Just then a mysterious middle-aged woman walked in. Adi hurriedly pulled up a chair for her, just like a true gentleman. She scanned Rob for a few seconds and shot Adi an icy glance. "Dr. Rosenberg! Thank you for coming at such short notice. This is Rob, my friend, we spoke about this afternoon."

"Hmm...very well," she said, passively scribbling notes on her pad.

Maya Rosenberg was the spearhead of this beta drug test. Without further ado, she made each one of them line up outside the lab door, taking the blonde woman in first. Her info sheet read 'Melissa Thorne, Age 22'. While waiting for his turn Rob's mind wandered from how the money could solve his rent issue, to Nadia's wellbeing. Tara had already filled him in with all the recent happenings, unbeknownst to Adi. Rob decided to press him for answers.

"Hey Adi… Bro…why the rush man?" Adi stopped in his tracks, giving Rob an exasperated look. "Haven't heard from your cousin these past few days? How's Nadia doing?"

Adi's ears turned red, flustered at how he never thought of hiding Nadia before bringing Rob on board. "She's at her colleague's place around the corner," he blurted out.

He couldn't think of a lamer excuse, thought Rob. "Hmm… I see, quite a last-minute plan I'd say," replied Rob deciding to play along. Adi knew that he had to keep Nadia well-hidden with Rob breathing down his neck. He shrugged Rob aside and proceeded to usher in Samuel. Rob thought hard, how could he rescue her, but first, where was she being held? He then noticed a staircase adjoining the bedroom wall, diagonally opposite to the kitchen. The kitchen area was adjacent to a large storage space that provided enough room to set up the lab. While Adi was busy, Rob decided to snoop around. He proceeded down the stairs and landed in a passageway. There were two bedrooms and a small dining area with only a microwave, for the participants.

"Nadia…" Rob whispered. "NADIA?!" He said in a louder tone. But there was no response. Rob somehow had a hunch she was being held there, but he couldn't be gone for too long. His turn was up next, so he quietly returned back to his spot.

Adi came to get Rob. This was his best chance to shift Nadia to a secluded place. He hurried down, lifted Nadia, from one of the bedrooms while still unconscious, and brought her to the upstairs bedroom. The walk-in closet was her new room. Adi was momentarily overcome with a sense of guilt, seeing the plight of his cousin, but what had to be done was done. Rob was so close to discovering Nadia, a slip-up Adi could not afford.

All three of them were done with the pre-tests. Rob and Samuel shared a room, while Melissa occupied the other room. Ken and Adi rotated between the upstairs bedroom and his apartment, while also keeping a watch on Nadia. Nadia's apartment bedroom was stocked with emergency medical equipment and the living area served as an office for Dr. Maya and her team to hold meetings just next door.

Later that night, Nadia was slowly gaining consciousness, the effects of the morphine were wearing off. Luckily Ken was on her watch and it was Nadia's mealtime. A few doors away, Rob decided to snoop again. He glided upstairs and found the bedroom door slightly ajar. He caught a glimpse of a frail girl, her back facing, eating a dry sandwich. *Is it Nadia?* he thought to himself. How disheveled she looked! Rob decided to pry further and stretched his arm toward the knob. Just then, he felt a hand on his left shoulder. Rob prayed hard that it wasn't Adi.

Chapter 11
By Kunal Sharma

Co-authors: Bhoomi Satwani, Pahul Khanija, Abdullah Ahmad, Aryaman Verma, Pranav Thomas

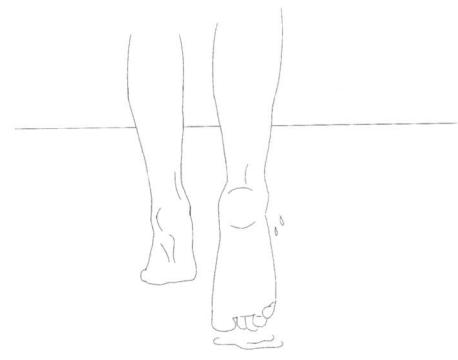

Illustrated by Lennita D'Coutho

Hot steam swirled around the tiny pale blue bathroom yet her feet flinched as they touched the cold ceramic tiles. Tara reached for the damp towel hanging behind the door dropping used and dirty clothes that hadn't seen the inside of a washing machine for weeks. She stood there shivering for a few moments as the water droplets fell around her. Taking a few steps toward the mirror Tara wiped her hand across its surface revealing red puffy eyes that stared back into hers. Her blonde hair looked dull and hung like soggy old noodles. Her face had definitely aged. Tara was exhausted and her attempt to wash away the last few hours had done little to ease the tension in her neck and shoulders.

Leaving tiny wet footprints from the bathroom to Rob's bedroom, Tara searched for something clean to wear. The last time she was in his room was almost exactly a year ago. If she tried hard enough maybe she would be able to find the puddle of puke she had left behind along with her self-respect after she had aggressively flung herself at Rob that night and he turned her down as gently as he could. Something about her being vulnerable after a funeral. Something about giving herself time to feel her mother's loss. The next thing she remembered was crying in Nadia's car. Then her lap where time appeared to stay still. After Tara's mother had succumbed to a long three-year battle with cancer, Nadia was the closest thing to family she had left. The sides of her mouth tugged into a small sad smile as she remembered their first encounter. As luck would have it, it seemed the student accommodation at their local university had quite the sense of humor to pair together two girls who couldn't be more different. Nadia was tall and slim, with an air of easy confidence and a magnetic pull that was irresistible to all around her. Tara had struggled with rolls around her waist all her life and the faster she ran toward things, the further away they got. Yet, they both found themselves in their little shared kitchen that first semester of university with no plans on Valentine's Day. Two bottles of champagne later (courtesy of Nadia's black credit card) the two girls covered everything from their past relationships, secrets they hadn't repeated even to their closest friends, and their hopes and aspirations. They shared pizza (no pineapples – they agreed that it was unacceptable as a topping), watched chick flicks, applied charcoal face masks, and laughed all the way through till the morning They were inseparable ever since.

Lately, however, there was a slight disconnect. A shift. It wasn't that Nadia ever made her feel that way but after university Tara felt a need to find a way out of Nadia's shadow. Putting herself out there as this quirky, body-confident girl online helped do wonders for her self-esteem and Nadia couldn't have been more proud of her best friend. But it made her distracted. Sometimes unavailable. It made Tara blush to think her ego could have jeopardized their friendship.

It was a little past 9 pm; only a couple of hours since Rob had left. Tara's leg tapped anxiously against the table. The sound matching the ticking of the clock in perfect tandem. Absentmindedly, she moved the cursor on Rob's computer, clicking at files, not really noticing the names until her eyes landed on a folder titled *Naddy*, Rob's nickname for Nadia.

This feels intrusive, thought Tara, the cursor hovering over the files. *Ah, screw it.* She double-clicked. Photos of Nadia covered the screen. Nadia laughing. Nadia pulling a funny face. Nadia lost in thought. Maybe photos Nadia wasn't even aware were being taken.

What the... What kind of creepy shit is this? thought Tara leaning in close to the screen. *Either he's just weirdly in love with her...or is he in on this whole mess? He believed my story so easily earlier today.* Tara rubbed her fists against her eyes in frustration until she saw spots. She didn't know what to believe anymore. *But, if he genuinely had something to hide, why would he just leave me here with access to his computer? Wouldn't I be back in that apartment with Nadia?*

She scanned the photos some more, both uncertain of what she was looking for and scared of what she might find. Did he have folders on all his friends?

As the thoughts in Tara's head fought with each other, a familiar notification bell rang out interrupting them. It was from her secret messenger. There was no text, just an attachment. Tara's heart was beating out of her chest as she clicked the video link. For a few moments the screen was blank. Then all of a sudden there she was. It was her from earlier today at the park. But in the video she was walking right up to the silhouette. She stood there for a few moments, reached down, and then sprinted away out of view. Someone had recorded her and doctored the footage. Right as the video ended, there was another message. *Turn on the news.*

Tara scanned the room for the remote and leaned to pick it up. Her hand touched the residue of many meals as she pressed down hard on the overused button to turn on the TV.

"Come on, come on, come on," Tara muttered under her breath. *Oh shit.* Flashed in bold across the screen were the words **Breaking News: Body found in Byde Park**. Tara recognized the red mass of hair instantly. It was the man from the park. He was dead. Tara watched the news uncover over the next few minutes in complete shock. No further information other than Aaron was a 43-year-old male who had been infected and was in the last stages of Budlyt and his body had been found at that exact park bench a little earlier today. His body had been discovered by a passing drone.

Her phone buzzed on the table. *We'll be in touch.*

Chapter 12
By Dinete Thomas

Co-authors: Winnieta Romell, Shaniah Rodricks, Ajay Kumar, Sheila Bugal, Arun Vijayan

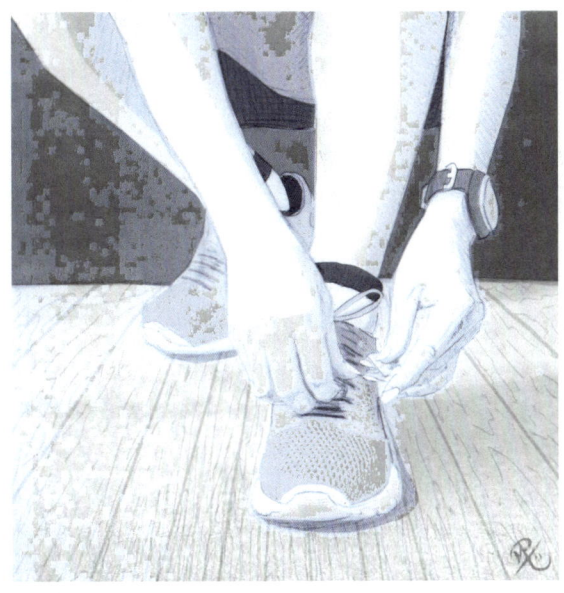

Illustrated by Mahesh Perera

The news of the body found in Byde Park was still sinking in. *It was definitely the same guy,* thought Rob. *Too many close calls.* The shocking announcement that came on the news right after he had just been told off by creepy old Samuel for wandering off when he should be resting made Rob feel like he had been too lucky for his own good. His lame excuse of trying to look for the cute blonde woman he saw while waiting to meet Dr. Rosenberg had left Samuel in peals of laughter as he sauntered off to bed. As Rob lay back down, he could feel his body twitching with nerves; he had finally found Nadia. Not more than 30 feet away, she lay looking far closer to dead than alive. As the drugs started to take effect, dark thoughts started to twirl around in his head, what if this was a suicide mission? Could he save the love of his life? Could he pull off the impossible and ride off into the sunset with Nadia? Would Adi catch onto them? Would Nadia survive the night? His head aching from the thoughts of a million different ways this plan would fail, Rob gave way to the pain and eventually passed out.

In a different room, Ken woke up, startled by the noise from the ECG Monitor and half realized he was still on watch duty for Nadia. After checking in to see if everything was okay, he slouched back into the couch, staring at her.

Good looks seem to run in the family, he thought. For as much of a hunk he was, Adi did have the edge over him to woo over anyone. *Smart and cocky too,* he mused. They had started out as interns together but their trajectory henceforth took them on different roads to the same destination. Sure, Ken was smart too. But the higher ups quickly realized his flimsy moral compass was much more valuable.

There she lay, her beauty depleting just as her health, injected with the same strain of the virus that was menacing the world. Cruel but needed, it was all for the greater good as

Adi has paraphrased it for the benefactor – the mysterious individual pulling the strings with Adi as his puppet. This was what they were working for; being the only ones with a cure.

So how was it possible that a simple pharmaceutical startup could compete and beat the race to a vaccine against the big pharma giants? This was nothing short of a Bond movie. Mysteriously highly respected scientists and medical professionals were starting to disappear all over the world. Unlucky accidents, alleged suicides, and some had even succumbed to the virus. Bit by bit their competition was slowly becoming as relevant as the zits on his chin. Every few days...*pop*.

Ken crossed his legs and closed his eyes in contentment. He was happy to be a part of the ride. His partner was driving and he was cruising along in the passenger seat, the top down, and doing just fine. He wondered what car he would get himself when this was all over.

A few doors away, Adi paced in frenzied zig-zags around his apartment. His sneakers squeaked at each abrupt turn sounding like he was playing back on his old high school basketball court. He stopped with his back to the news playing on mute on his 55-inch tv.

I cannot believe this is happening, he thought, fists balled up tightly against his sides. *Shit.* He slowly turned around. His sculpted face bathed in the blue light flashing from the screen, the light bounced carelessly over his features now tightened with anger and worry.

While Matana gaped at the lifeless body, gossiped about who the man was, and invented theories about his death, Adi already had the answers. Aaron Keen was ex LifaLabs (the pharma company they used as an invisibility cloak over their real operations) and he was damn good. He was notorious for being a little eccentric but his knowledge and passion taught Adi everything he knew. He took Adi under his wing and had turned into a mentor, maybe even as far as a paternal figure, for the young intern. When he had contracted the infection into their second month of research, he had fought their decision to rest and spend time with his loved ones. Aaron had to have a security escort out of the lab. The memory made Adi's blood boil. What he had laughed at and even admired about what he had believed to be Aaron's unwavering commitment to their cause was actually a big fat finger to Adi and the team and no one knew it. Until now. There it was on his wrist an unmistakable outline of a key designed with the makings of a motherboard tattooed into his pale skin. It had to be new. The reddened and swollen skin told him as new as a week or so. To the regular civilian, the tattoo could appear to be a drunken mistake that made for a funny anecdote or a youthful interpretation of an existential crisis. This particular tattoo however, symbolized, a pledge of allegiance and there all over Adi's screen was a vision of that unwavering commitment. *To someone else.* "Bloody rat!"

Adi let out one last growl at the screen then collapsed into a chair to think. They were sending a message. With every screen in Matana filled with closeups of Aaron, they would be heard loud and clear.

The ring of a Finsta notification made him jump.

I really need to get my shit together, Adi thought as he tapped to view the notification. It revealed to him information he had been waiting for. Tara was posting. An electric shiver made its way down his spine. Tara had finally made a mistake.

It would make it so much easier to track her down now. Adi threw on his sports jacket, bent to fix his left shoelace, grabbed his keys, and quickly typed out a text: *Be back soon. Time to tie up one loose end.*

Chapter 13
By Samad Khan

Co-authors: Kristelle Paciente, Joel Brennan, Laura Faumuina, Daksh Ramnani

Illustrated by Bhoomi Satwani

Tara's gaunt features glowed in the light of the street lamps passing by her in the car window. She was agitated and the cacophony of questions swirling around in her mind made her fill with confusion. She had received a text: *Trida Tower. Black Car. Plate M1631. One hour. You'll get your answers.*

Answers, she thought to herself. She couldn't remember the last time she had thirsted for answers. Likes and comments had given her all she needed: accolades, ego boosts, direction. She hadn't had a need for anything else.

Getting to the pickup location was hard enough without being spotted by the roving flocks of drones overhead...ducking through trees and backyards and avoiding main streets without having to come to terms with getting in a car to go to an undisclosed location to speak to a person who'd been sending strange messages. She looked up at the face of a man in a well-cut suit, a man who had been silent for the last ten minutes of their journey, a man whose features, much like his intentions, were shrouded in shadows, save for small intermittent panels of yellow light that flashed by too quickly to reveal anything more than a sharp piercing green gaze and dark brown hair pulled back into a long thick braid down his right shoulder. Tara shifted nervously on the leather seat, breaking the silence, and attempted to shrink back into the upholstery, then bracing herself, she opened her mouth and blurted out, "What the hell is going on?! Who are you? Look, Mr. Suitandtie, I'm over this, why have you been messaging me? What do you want from me?!"

The man slowly leaned forward, green eyes fully focused on Tara and his mouth in a stoic expression, "Tara, thank you for coming. My apologies but the subterfuge was necessary, Lifalabs has many operatives active in the area and between them and the heightened security measures due to lockdown, conventional methods of communication were deemed imprudent. We needed to get you away from the man you call

Adi." His voice rumbled into the darkness of the car and they sped down the back streets toward the factory belt on the outer edge of Matana; chimney stacks and cooling towers creating a jagged skyline, an oxymoronic testament to human progress.

Tara's mind reeled with an anxiety that was becoming uncomfortably familiar to her. Adi. The man she once knew as her best friend's older cousin seemed to be at the cause of it. How deep did this plot run? Where was Nadia? Would Rob get her out of there? Tara's eyes started welling up with tears, her chest felt like it was about to explode and she couldn't catch her breath. Her world was falling apart all around her. *Screw the fame, screw the virus,* she thought. All she wanted was her old life back, and Nadia. God knows what Adi has already done to her, was she even still alive?

Tara slumped forward, elbows on her knees and head in her palms.

"Let me introduce myself, Dorian Palmers, software engineer. I work for a private covert organization that is keen to overlook the Budlyt-19 vaccine efforts. Lifalabs is also engaged in the production of a vaccine, but it is in everyone's best interests if their efforts are derailed."

Silence filled the car, they had pulled up outside a heavily secured warehouse backed by a tall line of the forest. Tara was still slumped forward, unable to string thoughts together and convey the turmoil that was twisting inside her like a coiled snake. She felt sick and dehydrated and her legs ached from running. So much running. She was through running. Turmoil suddenly gave way to sharpness and clarity.

"You sound like you want to help, but your actions seem less than benevolent! Why doctor that video of me at Byde

Park? Seems a funny way to elicit someone's help with the use of threats, don't you think?" Tara's voice was shrill with what seemed like hysteria but was actually a sense of reckless abandon. She didn't care what was going to happen to her, all she wanted was Nadia back.

"Tara, I know how difficult this must be. But I need you to tell me everything you know about Adi, it might be the only way we can help Nadia. The video was only meant as a means to ensure your cooperation to come to this meeting with me and my benefactor. If the terms set don't meet your expectations, you can go free...but you will run the risk of losing your friend, the choice is yours."

Hearing these words, Tara felt caged again. On the one hand, she has just been offered the opportunity to save her friends, but the price was stepping into the unknown with this undertaker of a man. Something about him raised the hair on the back of her neck.

Tara stared at Dorian, completely aghast, as he wordlessly motioned toward the entrance of the warehouse which was guarded by hired guns. Dorian continued on his spiel on why Tara should be helping him as they walked through hallways made of crates piled to the ceiling. "Adi and Lifalabs are trying to make a hybrid of the virus and human DNA so that they can better study it and more easily find a cure, but our intel suggests that they also plan to weaponize a mutated strain for use in the military as a more lucrative venture. They care nothing for world health and well-being, they're opportunists just looking for profit."

Tara and Dorian stopped in front of a large set of metal roller doors which opened onto a large floor space teeming with men and women in lab coats all feverishly working toward a seemingly common goal. Tara thought some of them looked familiar, and Dorian noticed.

"You might have seen a couple of faces on the news, some of the many brilliant minds Lifalabs tried to extinguish in an attempt to consolidate all the patents they could for research into the virus. When the first few specialists started losing their lives, we knew we'd have to act quickly."

Secret organizations. Private labs. Rescued scientists. Where did this rabbit hole end?

Tara felt a hand squeeze her shoulder, "We aren't the bad guys, Tara, we're trying to help. And we need your help now."

Chapter 14
By Zaha Talibuddin

Illustrated by Neil Zuzarte

Tara followed Dorian through the warehouse as he explained every room and its relevance to their mission. Somewhere during Dorian's lengthy explanation of the logistics of his team and how they accessed LifaLabs' confidential files, which was complete with extensive and pretentious vocabulary, Tara's mind wandered to the thought of Rob and Nadia. She wondered if Rob had been successful in finding Nadia and assuring her that they were going to help her. Her mind spiraled into different theories about where they could be at this very moment and if Adi knew that Rob had been in contact with her. She pictured Rob finding Nadia and embracing her in an intimate hug. Her thought immediately darkened with the entrance of Adi, who hastily injected them both with some sort of swampy substance. Before she could come up with the next sequence of events, Tara tried to shake the awful thought. Realizing she had allowed her mind to wander off, which was in turn making her miss Dorian's explanation, she tried to tune back into what he was saying.

"—we then process that information on our state-of-the-art technological system to allow us to access their community of benefactors—"

"Why do you even need me?" Tara interrupted. "What help could I possibly provide that's more valuable than your 'state of the art technological processes?'" Tara asked in a tone intended to mock Dorian. She was losing her patience, one which was already limited. Tara had no interest in hearing about Dorian's company machines and how they worked. At that moment, she was only worried about Rob and Nadia. For the first time in years, Tara was allowing herself to prioritize the thoughts of people other than herself.

In order to understand Tara, one must know that she immersed herself in her social media presence to distract others from the emptiness in her life. Behind the screen, Tara was another lonely and insecure girl who felt the need to sugar-coat and glamourize her life so as to convince the world that she was happy. She hoped that one day this mask would morph into reality and she could become the version of herself that she presented to society. The only person who was ever able to see past her fake façade was Nadia. Now, her only concern was saving her friends, no matter what the consequences may be.

Dorian explained that apart from knowing everything about the predicament that Rob and Nadia were in, he was aware of their friendship with Adi, whom Dorian explained they had been monitoring since the beginning phase of the LifaLabs experiments.

"We've had our eyes on Adi Drubber for quite a while now. You see, Tara, Adi is just a kid who got caught up in the idea of saving the world. By the time he realized he had gotten himself involved with a dangerous crowd, it was too late to back out and too late to reach out for help. We feel that, with your support, we can convince Adi to help us by serving as someone who informs us about what happens on the inside of LifaLabs."

"Okay, hold it right there," Tara shouted. "How would you have even the slightest idea of what Adi wants? Trust me, he's no good guy. That guy has had a mask on for years now: pretending to be our friend when in reality he's letting all those innocent people suffer for a stupid experiment."

Acknowledging her concerns, Dorian said he had a way to prove that Adi was looking to escape the hold of the LifaLabs team. However, this plan could only materialize if Tara found a way to make Adi meet with her. Dorian explained that Adi would have to be under the impression that he had succeeded in finding Tara, whom he should think did not want to be found. Immediately, Tara was struck with the perfect idea. She had her doubts about Dorian and his company, however, when she weighed her options, the chance of Dorian and his company being able to help save Nadia and Rob outweighed them.

Tara anxiously asked Dorian if she could borrow someone's phone. Without hesitation, he reached into his pocket and gave her his. She opened the app store and downloaded Finsta. As she watched the tiny circle become full, indicating the app was downloading, she explained her plan to Dorian. A smile appeared on his face when he realized that Tara was helping lead Adi to her. Once the app downloaded, Tara logged into her account and quickly ran outside the warehouse to take a picture of herself. Without editing or assigning a thought-felt caption to the photo, she hit post.

She heard the sound of footsteps approaching her and quickly swiveled her head around to see Dorian. Before she could say anything, she watched as Dorian's eyes moved to look past her. Following his gaze, Tara noticed another man in a black suit. The man was avidly avoiding eye contact with Tara. Instead, his eyes like dark coals were burning back at Dorian to meet his gaze. Tara saw Dorian subtly nod his head at the other man; a small and smug smile emerged in the corner of his face.

Chapter 15
By Osman Khan

Illustrated by Mahesh Perera

Nadia awoke with a start.

Her skin felt clammy, covered with a light sheen of sweat. Stomach churning, she rolled over on her side. 3:42 am, the digital clock blinked back at her mechanically. Another sleepless night, another 24 hours in captivity, a familiar sinking feeling in her chest. Questions swirled around her mind.

Why had Adi abducted her? What was the nature of the experiments they were running on her? What drugs had been pumped into her system, and which ones were to follow? Who was Ken? More importantly – who was Adi behind the mask?

Sighing, she sat up feebly with what little strength she had. Thoughts of escaping had plagued her since her imprisonment had begun, but Nadia knew that she would only get one attempt – it was truly do or die when it came to escaping this nightmare. Straining her ears, she tried to figure out who was on duty tonight, Ken or Adi. Fragments of voices drifted up from down the hallway.

"…going to get…this has to finish… Tara has no idea… Keep an eye on…"

Adi. The smooth, husky voice was unmistakable. Nadia shuddered, recalling her childhood, playing with Adi at his parents' house.

"…don't worry…I'll make sure…the rest of the participants… Melissa, Sam, and Rob are…"

This one was Ken. His oily demeanor made its way into his voice. Again unmistakable.

Wait a minute. He just mentioned Rob. Was Rob here? Her friend Rob? What was Rob doing here? And it sounded like Adi was on his way out. The door slammed a second later. Silence. Nadia knew this was it. This was her chance.

Heart thudding in her chest, she swung her legs off the bed and tip-toed to the door. Pulling it fully open, she peeked out, both ways. Empty. Slipping into the hallway, she crept along, eyes wide open, ears peeled, prepared for the worst, but hoping for the best. The tiles gleamed almost unnaturally, as if reminding her that nothing that happened here would ever be public knowledge. A sterile operation. Done and dusted. Shaking, she moved past the first doorway, not bothering to check who was inside.

Then the second doorway.

Then the kitchen.

All of sudden, she heard the shuffling of footsteps coming up the stairs. Ken. He always dragged his feet when he was walking around, the Igor Strausman to Adi's Dr. Frankenstein. Frantically looking around, Nadia knew she had to hide, and had few options. Jumping on her toes backwards, she grabbed the knob to the second room, opening it a fraction and slinking through the narrow gap, closing her eyes in pure terror at being discovered. Behind her, she heard Ken making his way up the stairs, and entering the kitchen.

Opening her eyes, she saw that this bedroom didn't house any trial participants or equipment, but seemed like a home office. Shining glass top on the desk, state-of-the-art iCom. The screen was on; it seemed Adi had left in a hurry. It also seemed he had not anticipated Nadia walking into this room because on the screen, she saw...Lifalabs' logo winked at her at the top, and below, a medical file with her face on it.

Trembling, Nadia crept closer, her own smiling picture staring back at her. She reached out with a shaking hand and moved the cursor down, taking in the contents of the research that had been conducted on her over the past days against her will.

Name: Nadia Drubber

Alias: Subject 62

Age: 27

Sex: Female

Budlyt-19 Status: Positive

Research notes: Subject 62 first identified by Adi Drubber on March 27th as a potential target. Brought in for testing to Lifalabs Remote Facility Alpha on March 30th. On April 1st, Subject 62 was injected with a lethal dose of Budlyt-19. So far, Subject 62 has exhibited none of the signs of infection. No slowing of lung operations, no loss of taste or smell, no cardiovascular irregularities. For reference, Subjects 1 through 61 had to be placed on ventilators, monitored 24/7 and eventually disposed of. Preliminary conclusion: She is the key to marrying the RNA of Budlyt-19 to human DNA and creating both a vaccine and a weaponized virus. Further testing is recommended.

Nadia felt her knees buckle beneath her. She gripped the side of the desk to keep her balance and gazed in shock at the screen. Her world seemed to be turning inside out, her mind racing with questions behind her stunned silence; new questions that thundered through her mind and erasing the previous ones about Adi and Ken.

Was she infected? But she couldn't feel anything. She wasn't displaying any symptoms. What about the Subjects before her, who succumbed to the virus? Lifalabs were trying to weaponize the virus through human DNA? And she was the key – was she…immune?

Footsteps. The door creaked open. She whirled around.
"Rob?!"

Chapter 16
By Aleena Mansoor

Illustrated by Bhoomi Satwani

What unprecedented times, thought Adi as he drove, whizzing past the glittering wanna-be utopia that was Matana.

She is immune. Who would have thought, mused Adi, massaging the thought in his mind, the same words curdling since the moment he had made the chilling discovery. Even as he raced to ambush Tara, he could not help but map out the implications of what this could mean. Adi had not dared to share this information with Ken or his big-boss – it had to be deployed, manipulated, and executed in a precise manner.

Adi's lips curled up in one corner, making his usually handsome face look almost manic and depraved.

"Oh the possibilities," he said aloud with no witnesses other than the steadily increasing numbers on his flickering speedometer – 100, 150, 200. Here he thought that creating a military-grade bio-weapon was all he was good for, but in his hands also lay the antidote. Images of bleeding noses, sullen-eyed enemy soldiers struggling to hold the gun as they aimed to shoot Matana soldiers, flashed, making Adi almost sneer in glee. They could even sell it to all their allies, they would be rolling in cash. What made the symphony even more poetic, was not just the havoc they could create to protect Matana, but the order they could institute. Be the only antidote in the world, under the name of a self-created and owned pharmaceutical company to deploy at will where it deemed fit. Be the problem and the solution at the same time, double the trouble, double the gains. It would be a powerful tool of diplomacy, even more precious than oil and the world would be at Matana's feet…as it should be. He could almost see the monument erected in his honor, "Just hope they get my hair right, it's hard to sculpt curls."

A billboard passed "Glory to Matana" it said with the President of Matana posing artificially with a bright, forced smile that was reserved purely for photo ops, his stomach bulging out of his 3-piece pin-striped suit. A random memory flashed in his mind; he and Nadia always took this route to the gym, "You know Adi, one would hope they'd have our President's back when photographing him, just look at the poor guy!"

Adi would chortle, "All I know is that the size of his gut reminds me why we are going to the gym, I take it as positive reinforcement," with Nadia breaking into infectious giggles while she schooled him for being a jerk.

Oh Nadia. Beautiful, kind Nadia, the closest person he had to a confidante since his childhood. When his parents died in that ill-fated car crash, she was the only one who would know not to ask him questions but sit with him in silence, sometimes curling her entire hand around a single finger of his – another ridiculous but somehow perfect gesture to show she understood his need for space, but would be there when he resurfaced.

Sadness fell like a curtain, the speedometer flickering to a 100. When had he become this monster? He had never really meant to kill people, he was doing this for Matana! Wasn't he? Okay for the money and power too, but he had never meant for Nadia to get caught in the cross-hairs. *Why did she have to be so god-damned curious,* he thought, banging the steering wheel, she was always so precocious. And now for her to be the antidote, it made it so much harder for him to not leverage this. Power was the only form of control he knew since his parents' death had quaked his life. He needed it.

The car neared what appeared to be some darkened warehouses, he could make out a ghost of some parked SUVs in the dead of the night. "Where the heck are you, Tara? There seems to be nothing Finsta-worthy here."

He felt a sick clenching in his heart. Something was wrong. No, this didn't make sense. Different possibilities whirred in his mind.

"Abort Mission," he mumbled, changing gears and reversing in full speed. In the rearview mirror, he caught an entourage of vehicles with bright headlights speeding towards him. *Shit.* He changed gears again accelerating in the opposite direction but the battalion of parked SUVs switched their headlights on in one fell swoop, blinding him. Peeking with one eye open he saw Tara's tiny frame jump out of one of the SUVs. "Dorian! That's him," she yelled out.

Out of the other SUV, Dorian stepped out along with the man in a perfectly manicured black suit. Adi could not make out his face, "These goddamned lights." The suited man walked closer to his car, blocking out one of the lights aimed directly into Adi's eyes.

Adi felt all the air leaving his lungs, his eyes peeled, almost manic. "Dad?" he whispered.

Chapter 17
By Benjamin Ralson

Co-authors: Mahesh Perera, Roman Krilov, Dinesh Sharma, Karan Mathur

Illustrated by Nishant Mishra

"Oh, God!" Rob's heart stopped before whispering glibly, "I knew you'd be fine," as if he had already forgotten his morbid thoughts from mere minutes ago. He drank in every detail of her appearance and couldn't help but compare her eyes to those of a scared deer who sensed danger was nearby. Big dark pools filled with distrust and vulnerability.

Nadia, still reeling from the realization that Adi saw her as a pawn in his amoral capitalist pursuits, allowed herself a glimmer of hope before hissing, "Rob, what are you doing here!?"

Her ephemeral relief was quickly replaced with cynicism. How could she trust anyone? Was Rob in cahoots with her cousin? How did those closest to her pose the biggest threat? The waves of uncertainty crashed against her like an existential dread that would inevitably drown her.

As Rob briefed Nadia on his and Tara's schemes, her mistrust began to evaporate as quickly as it set in. Rob, simple Rob, was nothing like Adi. She felt her heart unclench in her chest and her body loosen. After allowing herself a moment to let the past few days sink in she released an exhausted sigh. But there was still so much that lay ahead.

"Rob, you need to see these files immediately."

As they pored over the research notes, the color from Rob's face drained. Nadia searched his demeanor for any form of emotional response, but she could only find disbelief. Nadia's sanity temporarily wavered as she waited for something from Rob. *Anything*.

"Say something, please," she muttered cautiously.

"This runs deep, Nadia. We don't know who else is involved in this. We need to be careful," Rob sagely offered while Nadia glanced at him peculiarly. "This could be orchestrated by the government – or worse..." *Aliens,* Rob's thought trailed off. *Am I still kind of high?* Rob became immersed in his own substance-damaged imagination for a moment before displaying the mental acuity required to free himself. He was grateful his tongue pushed back against vocalizing his paranoia.

"We need to send these to Tara," Nadia's brow furrowed as she spoke with a sudden intensity hitherto unseen by Rob. "Where is she – do you have your phone?"

"I-I ha-had to give it up to get in here," Rob conceded as he visibly grew distressed by his failure to plan out the minutia needed to impress Nadia. *Think*, Rob, *think*, he demanded of himself as his thoughts grew quicker and less coherent. He had managed to find Nadia; surely, he would be able to get them out of this. Maybe he could try and steal a phone from one of the people working here? *Forget it.* The thought was dismissed almost as soon as he had it. He had better chances of winning the lottery.

Nadia's voice groaned with the realization that she had no means of contacting Tara without Rob's phone. "Where is it? Are you able to get to it?" Nadia's thoughts returned to her ostensible immunity to Budlyt-19. *What could this mean? Am I still contagious to others? To Rob?*

In a sudden effort to maximize her ever-diminishing strength and cognizant of no alternative, she motioned to Rob. "We don't have a choice. We have to get out before they realize I'm missing." Nadia's eyes narrowed as she explained to Rob that she was always being watched.

As Rob crept out of the room, Nadia grasped his arm with a tightness that belied her lithe figure. "Wait, the others – the subjects – do they know?" She paused before adding, "Are they aware of what's happening here or are they like me?"

Rob cocked his head, *An uprising of the proletariats…* he pondered before abandoning that thought. "You're right, Naddy, this could be our ticket out of here." A moment of grandiosity swept across him before vanishing into thin air. Rob glanced at Nadia nervously. "From what I gathered, some are here for the easy money – that's how I convinced Adi to let me join."

Rob looked down and muttered, "Some have sick family members and are here out of desperation to help find a cure." He pushed those bleak thoughts to the back of his mind and breathlessly added, "What do we do?"

Together, they formulated a plot to return to their beds for the night, and tomorrow, slowly inform their co-inhabitants of their discoveries. Strength in numbers would be their force out of here. *But who could they trust?* Figuring that out would be step 1. Then a plan to rush their way out without anyone getting hurt. Step 2 would be much harder. If against all odds they were able to miraculously pull it off, only then would they be able to contact Tara.

And then what? Go to the police? A journalist who would believe them? Shout their story on news?

As Rob crept back to his bed, he felt Ken's voice surround him, chilling him to his core, "Is everything OK, Rob?" Rob's breathing intensified as he turned around and saw Ken's silhouette in the corner, heightened against the pale-yellow light filling the hall. "You seem jumpy, Rob," Ken's sardonic smirk revulsed him, "don't forget, the trial begins bright and early tomorrow. I hope you're ready."

Chapter 18
By Rakesh Mohan

Co-authors: Karan Bhatia, Ravi Sabnani, Salal Nasir, Zain Rashaad, Deepika Yadav

Illustrated by Amirali Nancey

Adi was pacing up and down the hall, annoyed about never being let into the study. The dark mahogany door was a thing of beauty as well as constant nightmares. Leaning against the door, all he could hear was silence broken by the occasional grunt or sighs of frustration. Frustration that paled in comparison to his. He never really understood what his dad got up to behind those doors.

Adi continued to pace, faster, stopping arbitrarily to press his ear hard against the cool wood. Silence, again. His curiosity discontented, an itch began to form around a single angry hive on his neck.

The sound of the bell rang across the house, followed by a young girl shouting out Adi's name. His favorite cousin was home for their playdate, at least this would take his mind off his father holed away in his study.

"Stop being so grumpy and bring out the Dulo board, I've missed seeing you lose," said a young chirpy Nadia. Adi was as sore a loser as they came, and their intense Dulo games heated up with occasional childish tantrums. Just as they were finishing up, the sound of the doorbell rang again. When Adi opened the door, his jaw fell in awe. He had only watched Tarzan on the TV and now he had one suited up standing right in front of him.

"May I speak with your father please?" asked a youthful Dorian, his braid long and thick like a twisted horse mane. His dark reflector shades hid half of his strong angular face. Before Adi could respond, he saw his dad rush past to greet Dorian as his mom followed quickly behind, running her hand nervously through her long hair as they chatted on the cold concrete footsteps of their simple suburban home. A few moments later the door shut. Their blue family van turned the corner and was never seen again.

That memory of his parents was something that would wake him up in cold sweats years into his adult life. Something he never admitted to anyone, not even to Nadia. It was a full day later when Nadia's mom got the dreaded call that Masha and Talal had gotten into a terrible car crash. His dad's body mutilated beyond recognition and only traceable from a DNA test. His mother's passing in a hospital bed a short while after. His beautiful mother and powerful father were no more alive than their bed in which they had laid their heads. The bed which Adi would sometimes sneak into when he had a bad dream and wanted to feel their secure warmth like a shield around him. There was nothing left from that memory but cold sheets.

Everything that followed was a blur. It was a surreal feeling for a young boy to be greeted with strange words he had never heard before by friends, family and strangers at the funeral. Being surrounded by people who he had never even seen before wailing as if it were their own parents lying feet away from them. Contending with the meaning of death, the meaning of being an orphan. Nadia next to him holding his hand in that familiar, warm way saying everything that needed to be said as her tiny fingers tried to grip his hand, as though trying to keep him from literally falling apart.

He couldn't even give them a proper goodbye, and neither could anyone else as they walked past the white closed casket with those ugly pink flowers draped all around. He hated those flowers. Throughout all this, he never shed a tear. All he kept doing was replaying the final moment he saw his parents get into the car with that Tarzan man.

It was nearly a week after the funeral that Adi could muster the courage to step foot into his dad's now empty study. Several men had drifted in and out during and after the funeral, taking away all its containments. He sat in the middle of the room and if he closed his eyes he could almost like a seance conjure the familiar sights and smells that now haunted this room. This is where it had all began, devouring any and all information he could. Several confidential and top-secret government documents, books on philosophy, and print outs of radical extremist views, and the whole lot. He would sneak away pages of anything that he could and read under the covers. Not understanding much of the contents and even less still of the man who wrote them and him into existence. Maybe it was the loss of his parents that subconsciously turned him into versions of them.

But now as he stared directly into the face of a ghost, Adi could only hear the sound of his own heart thumping in his ears. He didn't know if it was the rain or tears streaming down his face. His father was now inches from him and as he spoke Adi's heart came to a stop. "I'm sorry I never said a proper goodbye, but, it's good to see you again, my dear boy."

Chapter 19
By Niki Alex

Co-authors: Kaavya Suresh, Anirudh Suresh, Veena Sunil, Govind Menon, Sneha Menon

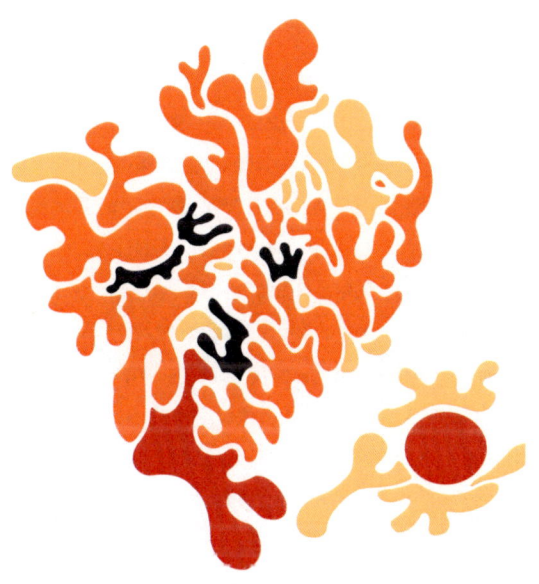

Illustrated by Arman Iqbal

Rob tossed around in dampened sheets watching the clock tick toward the crack of dawn. Was he stupid to think he could pull it off? The sheer audacity of their plan only seemed to worsen his anxiety and Ken's slimy reminder about the trials kept playing over and over in his head as he tried to figure out a change in their plan.

There was no alternative. He needed to get to the others. He rattled his brain thinking hard about their brief introductions and felt beads of sweat rolling down his back. *But who should I speak to?* His decision would severely alter their safety and his number was almost up. Do or die. This was what it must feel to engage in a reckless game of Russian roulette. If only his brain would cooperate. *Think*, Rob urged himself, *think!*

Rob sat up in his bed, his eyes closed, his fingers pressed deeply against his temples. Salt and peppered Samuel looked honest and open enough. He was warmer and more approachable than the 22-year-old barbie, Melissa, who seemed to want to keep to herself. As he tried to stitch together fragments of their fleeting conversation in the kitchen, Rob fought against a wave of questions drowning his already addled brain. One thing at a time. Who was here for the money? Who was here for a sick relative? Would either of them care if he told them their lives were in danger? Was this their last resort? Were any of them secretly in on this sick experiment and turn them in the moment he started talking about the plan? Could he barter Nadia being the cure in return for their escape? What were the answers?! The plan was seemingly turning into a suicide mission for everyone except for Nadia, he thought, how apt that she was immune to the virus. His life was one big punchline.

He looked up at the wall clock ticking away carelessly a few feet above him. He had about an hour left. *I'm screwed.*

Okay, enough. Time to start moving. Rob crept toward the entrance of his door and poked his head out. Samuel and Melissa were not far away and he couldn't hear much except the gentle *tick tick tick* reminding him he had a decision to make. *Fast.*

Rob scanned the room for something he could use to overpower Ken or even the other subjects if it came to it. He wasn't a particularly violent guy but at this moment his mind was scanning through a catalog of items in the room, selecting contenders to accompany him down the hall. His shoes? No. Everything else was too heavy. His eyes landed on a single glass lying on the side table, catching the moonlight, winking conspiratorially at him. His trembling hand clenched tightly around it.

He stopped and rehearsed what he would say. He had to make sure he didn't leave anything out or didn't come across as completely insane. *Of course this is insane! This whole thing is straight out of a bad horror movie.*

Okay, it's now or never.

He slowly placed one foot in front of the other, his ears straining for any sound he was responsible for. Or worse, Ken. His palm felt wet with sweat and his grip tightened around the glass. He held so tight he was worried it would shatter in his hand. Rob was directly outside their room now. He placed his head against the door for any indication that someone might be awake inside. Silence. His legs felt weak. His heart was sounding alarms in his chest and his blood was coursing hot through his body.

Rob took a deep breath, turned the doorknob, and entered the room.

Chapter 20
By Leanne Price

Co-authors: Allison Price, Nethmi Piyadigamage, Sarah Price

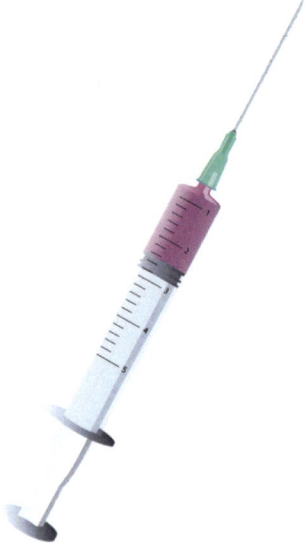

Illustrated by Arman Iqbal

Their beds were empty. How could they be empty? Anxiety riddled Rob as he scrambled to formulate another strategy. *Did they escape? Has Ken locked them away like Nadia?* The plan was falling apart already and it was up to a screw-up like him to fix it. He was never meant to be the hero. He wasn't good enough, using anything he could to avoid the world. Until now. Rob inhaled deeply and snuck back into the hallway. There were several doors in the hallway. Certificates of achievement from a likely fake company lined the glossy walls. Even in the dark the superficial nature of the facility still managed to disturb him.

After inching his way along the corridor, he was finally met with a sliver of light from an ajar door. Ken's voice was unmistakable.

"Alright, Melissa, you can go first. I'm sorry to wake you so late, but there's been a slight change of plan."

Rob leaned into the opening of the door. Melissa was being injected with a dark purple liquid. There was a file on the desk, obstructed from Samuel's and Melissa's view. It read **SUBJECTS M22 AND S24 TO BE TESTED WITH BATCH 6787, EXTRACTED AND REFINED FROM SUBJECT N. HYPOTHESIS – PHYSICAL CAPABILITIES TO BE ENHANCED.** Panic spread over Rob's body as he realized why Samuel and Melissa were being tested. Ken and Adi must have discovered another use of Nadia's 'testing.' Soldiers. Nadia may have been able to create not only a weapon, but the army to go with it.

Within seconds of the injection, Melissa began to convulse.

"Help me!" she cried.

Ken watched mercilessly as Samuel was frozen in horror. Her veins began to pop out, black stems spreading across her body like a wildfire. *Was she getting bigger?*

"Why…won't…you…help…me?" Melissa growled, her rage consuming her. She lunged for Ken, but he slid out of the way, leaving Samuel in her path. Melissa slammed into Samuel, then into the wall, breaking it. He slumped to the floor, motionless. Melissa began convulsing again, her eyes turned completely black. Unbeknownst to Ken, she locked eyes with Rob, her anger replaced with fear.

"Help me."

She fell to the ground, her eyes returning to normal and the black stems retreating. Ken bent over, checked their pulses and took notes on his pad. Melissa twitched feebly before Ken's apathetic eyes. Seconds felt like hours as Rob looked on, but soon enough her body became dormant. *Were they even still alive?* Rob could only watch in horror as Ken injected Samuel with the same dark purple liquid.

Samuel shot up, the same black stems and eyes emerging. He fixated on Ken. "What's happening to me?" Life did not flash before you like all the films portrayed but rather a sensation of disbelief followed by panic which was relayed in slow motion. All these thoughts passed as quickly as a breath.

"Well, Samuel, given your lack of convulsions and sudden rage, I'm guessing the serum was more successful on you. Unfortunately poor Melissa will need to be hospitalized. It seems to be that everyone reacts differently. I hope that you will be a more successful test."

Samuel began to stagger towards Ken.

"You can't do this, I don't feel right." With sweat starting to build, and goosebumps protruding from his arms, Samuel realized that the vaccine may all be part of a master plan. "This was supposed to be the vaccine. What is this?"

Samuel convulsed heavily and reached for Ken, missed, and put his fist on the desk, splitting it in half.

"I wouldn't worry, Samuel, it seems to me that you are about to be another unsuccessful test." Samuel tumbled to the ground, landing in front of Rob. Ken watched Samuel fall and met eyes with Rob. Ken smiled menacingly. He pulled another syringe out of his pocket.

"Now, I wonder what this will do to you."

Chapter 21
By Soraya Khan

Co-authors: Akash Vaswani, Arman Mohammed Iqbal, Ziyad Bangara

Illustrated by Lennita D'Coutho

Adi's mind swam with fragmented emotions, an unrelenting clamor of dashed assumptions and old memories. Realizing he hadn't taken a breath, he drew a shuddering inhale, feeling his chest fill with the icy night air. Raindrops trickled down a heavy brow furrowed over those glinting eyes as Talal, Adi's father, motioned with his head toward Dorian.

As Dorian moved toward an SUV to retrieve something from the back seat, Adi saw Tara's face illuminated in the window when the door opened. Their eyes met and her expression twisted with dread. She set him up. She set HIM up. His mind suddenly sharpened and he no longer stood with weak knees. He remembered why he was there and could feel his own insides writhing in rage at not realizing the now obvious and poorly planned subterfuge. Eyes darting from SUV to surrounding personnel, to terrain and escape routes, Adi feverishly tried to formulate a plan to extract Tara from this ambush situation.

Talal felt Adi's posture shift and swiveled his head back around, "Adi-*ARGH!*" Talal's head snapped back as he felt Adi's fist connect with his jaw, losing his grip on Adi's shoulders, "ADI WAIT!"

Adi ran swiftly toward the SUV, eyes fixed on Tara, a dead and maniacal expression on his face as he dodged one shrouded figure and punched another in the gut, bringing it down in a crumpled heap. All the while he was honing in on Tara.

Dorian moved around to intercept Adi, now having dropped the coat he was sent to retrieve in favor of what looked like a remote car lock. As he stood between Adi and Tara, he calmly and loudly stated, "There's an easier way than this, you know, why use fists at a family reunion?"

Adi let out a gut-wrenching bellow as he ran toward Dorian with balled fists and tears streaming down his face. Dorian braced himself, eyes locked with Adi's, and quickly dodged a punch, left then right, moving nimbly to avoid Adi whose swings were becoming clumsy due to his desperation. He quickly backed off as Adi jumped into the driver seat and floored the accelerator and bolted for the open road without checking for a pursuit.

He twisted in his seat and leered at Tara as she cowered in the back seat trying to make herself as small as she possibly could, "You've given me quite the runaround, huh? HUH?!" The car swerved and he turned back around to watch the road, "Not to worry, there's a whole theme park of delights back at the apartment that I can't wait to test out on you!"

Tara whimpered pitifully as the SUV sped down the dirt track back toward the main city center, scratching at the door locks and dry sobbing as she fought to get free, all the while Adi's taunts were ringing through her mind. She began hyperventilating as she continued to desperately claw at the door handle to no avail. Adi sporadically checked on her through the rear-view mirror. His eyes were wide and manic.

Suddenly, the backseat partition flew up, obstructing Tara from view and doors locked shut with a mechanical snap. The car began to slow down to a rolling speed. He looked in the side mirror and noticed headlights rapidly approaching him from behind. "NO! What's happening?" he struggled to speed up but the car eventually came to a stop and all he could do was hammer at the windows to no avail. He then saw Tara slip out the passenger door and slumped back in his seat,

"Freaking family reunion it is," as he saw Talal jogging up from one of the parked cars now encircling them once again.

Talal peered into the driver's window, still rubbing his jaw. "Didn't count on those anti-theft precautions, did ya, sport! Still stubborn, just like when you were a kid, better at throwing punches though!" He chuckled and waved the car remote in his hand. Adi spat on the window in response. Talal's face dropped and hardened, "Look, Adi, I know this is hard to deal with, but nothing will be accomplished by fighting. You will be taken back to headquarters and you and I are gonna have a little chat."

After a difficult extraction from the stolen SUV, Talal, followed by Dorian and Tara and a now sedated Adi, sped back to their warehouse headquarters. Once they were all secure and inside a detainment room, Talal and Adi were left staring silently at each other from across one another at a table, alone.

Talal broke the silence first, "I know this is a lot but hear me out and I know you'll be—"

"Screw you," Adi began to chant.

"Adi, this is much bigger than you can imagine, please listen to me. That day, when your mother and I left, we were on our way to the Ministry of Health to present our findings. We were close to successfully developing a living bionic microorganism capable of self-replication and being controlled by humans. It was a remarkable breakthrough that we planned to use in the fabrication of a kind of broad-spectrum viral cure, capable of neutralizing the viral load in the person's bloodstream by directly attacking the offending virus. We called it Edenseed."

Adi continued to stare blankly into his father's pleading eyes. He was in some sort of a haze, he couldn't fully encompass what was happening around him.

"—and your mother would have done anything—"

Adi snapped back into focus, "Where's Mom?" Adi asked. He was almost afraid of the answer. "Why didn't you come back? What happened to you two?" Tears filled Adi's eyes and he was once more a young boy desperate for his father's approval.

Talal's face belied his broken heart as he spoke, "Your mother died in the car that day though Dorian and I survived. But it was no accident that took her from her family. This was a murder committed by a group of people who were bent on Edenseed not reaching its full potential...ALL IN THE NAME OF CAPITALIST GREED!" He slammed the table as he spoke, eyes ablaze and voice trembling with poignant rage. Adi looked at his father and finally saw a familiar face, one he desperately needed to be close to.

In a voice now calm like the air before a storm, Adi asked his father, "Who murdered my mother?"

Talal looked Adi straight in his eyes and replied, "That would be your employers, LifaLabs."

Chapter 22
By Avish Patel

Illustrated by Nishant Mishra

Back at the Lifalabs' apartment, Ken lunged toward Rob, syringe dripping with the purple liquid in hand. Rob went into fight or flight mode; his pupils dilated, vision in portrait, and with the world becoming sharp around the edges, he dodged Ken's advances and took off down the hallway. As he ran all he could hear was Ken screaming after him. Rob stumbled near the stairs, and felt a grab at his leg. He turned and saw Ken trying to inject him. With a look of panic on his face Rob screamed, aimed his foot at Ken's nose, kicking him square in the face. Rob felt a graze but was free from Ken's hold, he shot to his feet, and bolted up the stairs. As he emerged into the waiting area, he saw the locked apartment door in front of him.

Rob accelerated and without hesitation he dropped his shoulder, closed his eyes, and exploded through the door. Broken pieces of timber were strewn around him as he fell to the floor. Fight or flight mode. Heart racing and blood streaming from the splinters on his face, Rob gathered his senses and slowly climbed to his feet. In the hallway outside the apartment, he gathered pace and headed toward the lift. As he approached he glanced back and saw Ken emerge through the remnants of the door syringe in hand, dripping purple, nose broken with blood splattered down his shirt from the swift boot to the face moments earlier.

Rob ran past the lift and straight to the emergency stairwell, where he flew down the stairs losing count of how high up they were. He could hear the footsteps and calls of Ken coming down behind him. Rob burst through the emergency exit into the bright hot sun outside. He stopped. His brain in overdrive, with adrenaline rushing through his body he spun around and faced the door. Sweat dripping, mixing with the blood coming from his cheeks, he ignored the numbing pain in his face. Rob quickly rolled the apartment dumpster in front of the door, blocking it. Just as he had it in position, he heard a hard thump against the door. Ken. He heard Ken yell out, inaudible, and in frustration.

Rob had escaped, but as his heart slowed he realized he had left the others behind. Nadia was still there. He knew he had to go back for her. And Samuel. And Melissa. He spotted a lone drone flying in the distance. He jogged toward the back alleys and mentally mapped out the quickest way to get back to his apartment without being spotted. A few moments later Rob slowed down outside a pharmacy, tempted to step in, get a fresh batch of syrup to ease his pounding heart but for the first time in a long time Rob wanted to remain clear-headed. Fifteen minutes later, a panting Rob was outside his 5-story apartment complex. As he impatiently paced the length of the lobby waiting for the elevator, he prayed that Tara was home waiting for him.

Chapter 23
Rebecca Khan

Illustrated by Mahesh Perera

Somewhere high above the cityscape of Matana, warm yellow lights shone out of the windows of the penthouse suite. Tessellated window shutters and sheer flowing drapes revealed luxuriously appointed quarters, white fur throws on couches, covered gold silken upholstery, displays of expensive pottery, and in the middle of the room, a large desk made of solid black granite that featured crystal glasses and a decanter filled with liquor that glinted invitingly in the firelight.

From behind a large screen, one slender hand with long fingers covered in rings reached into the desk top drawer to pull out a pack of menthol cigarettes. Icy green eyes framed by long wavy blonde hair glowed as a match stick flared and a long plume of smoke enveloped the screen. Bracelets tinkled as Charlotte resumed typing, the screen covered in financial figures and calculations.

Heavy wooden doors pushed open and a smiling maître de walked in carrying a plate of food under a silver cloche and set it down next to Charlotte, "Compliments from the chef, Miss Yoss, a new shipment of abalone was just flown in from Javar, very popular this time of year." Without waiting for a response, he glided out of the room, leaving Charlotte to ruminate over her figures, "…and net profit is estimated to be…?" She said, clicking the mouse and smiling as the bottom line filled with zeros.

Staring out the window at the skyline, she stepped into a white pant suit then poured herself a glass from the decanter, "This cesspool city, so sleepy, so peaceful…they won't know what hit them." She sighed with contentment and sipped, "This backwater town, it's people, the world…they all thought I couldn't make it. Now look at them, writhing in their own filth while the government bungles around trying to contain this beautiful chaos. May it all burn to the ground."

Charlotte walked out onto the balcony and continued to stare downward, eyes falling on the private driveway that lead directly to a hidden entrance to the building, a direct line to the elevator in her suite. The path was suddenly illuminated by multiple headlights.

Charlotte felt her phone buzz and answered a call from her assistant, "Miss Yoss, your prospective clients have arrived, they're being shown to the board room now on the floor below…shall I tell them you'll be with them shortly?"

Charlotte replied, "Yes Shaun, thank you. I'll make my way down now."

Quickly snatching up papers in a folder marked, "Seeker, Cure" she made her way to the private elevators down to the floor where the meeting was being held. Elevator doors opened into a long hallway with warm colors on the walls, hanging art, and wooden floors, and Shaun, carrying a neat set of folders meant for the clients to follow during the meeting. Heels clacking down the hallway without hesitation, Shaun running ahead of her to open the boardroom doors, Charlotte stepped confidently in and greeted her clients, an array of fat men with ugly jewelry and expensive suits and wreaking of cigar smoke and cologne. Shaun quickly began passing out the folders, setting them down on each man's right side.

"Welcome, gentlemen, to LifaLabs…" she said smiling widely "…my name is Charlotte Yoss, sole benefactor of LifaLabs, and I have the big bad toys you boys want to play war games with." She snuggly grinned, seeing their bulging eyes light up. "What say we make a start on negotiations? Bidding starts at one billion US dollars, do I have any takers?" she smiled as the room erupted with offers and counter offers and started counting the number of islands she could buy.

Chapter 24
By Jeremy Nelson

Illustrated by Channon D'Souza

Alone in the fluorescent detainment room sat Adi, cheap tea in front of him from a vending machine that Talal had brought him. It was the least he could do to not overly upset his son to the point of his sanity dissipating like a passing mist. Only when this mist passes, it does not reveal the sun; it only drags behind it the night without blazing stars. The tea steamed gently from between his ever-increasingly shivering hands as a mirage clouded over his mind.

Had he known his company, for which he worked, killed his mother, would he have dared come this far? Or to even concoct the idea of working for them? Maybe things would have been different. But this was not possible. There was no alternate universe he could be swept up to, or a portal to walk through. His mother was dead. No other truth remained. But his father…

The mirage grew stronger now, more than palpable in the material of memories. His mind brought forward the memory of that day. From waking to the break of dawn to spending a long sleepless night at her bedside. Throughout that night, he only ever left for the toilet. Whenever he came back, he always expected her to be alive, sitting up on her pillow. But it was only the light on his eyes playing wicked tricks. The restroom was brighter than the dark hospital room after all. Whenever he thought she had moved, he was a lit firework, ready to explode in exultation. But with the minutes that passed of her eyes never opening came the rain. First a single drop, then a stream. No song swung sweetly up from her silent lungs. His father was already pronounced dead a little earlier, his body mangled beyond recognition, so the grief in his heart was unimaginable.

Adi remembered her calling after him walking to school as she watched him from the car. Talal worked around the clock so Adi's memories with his father were quite fewer than with his mother. Who could blame him? 'The world is your oyster, little robin. Make it what you see it worth.' He always remembered her calling him 'little robin.' It was because Adi was not big for his age but never let his confidence falter. To his mother, he was a brave resourceful fighter who had an air of ambition about him. He heard her say it in his dreams, whenever he had them in his house, in the dark perpetual nights of suburban Matana. Last time he had heard her haunting his dreams was not too long ago. 'Little robin. Little robin. Little robin,' she called. To this Adi would awake in a cold sweat, and not long after would he call, quietly, in a weak voice which exposed his still mourning; "Mama?"

Adi always tried his best to be strong, especially emotionally. It never got in the way of his work. In fact, he was rather slightly pedantic as far as hiding goes, and that started at his parents' funeral. It was in glorious sunshine that day. Fresh from a night in storms. So glorious was the sun that the black clothes the mourners wore almost had color to them. But what was brighter than the fire in the sky were their coffins. Pure white snowdrops and a presence filled the chapel when it was placed at the front for all to see. It was never opened, but Adi could feel them in it. Cold and alone. Her. It was his mother he was always closer to. He still couldn't believe she was gone.

At the side of the dugout grave, a headstone had already been set at the end of the long, oblong hole, they all stood in a circle as both the white coffins were lowered. The mourners were double in number compared to a normal funeral. A party for Adi's new orphan status, it seemed like to him. In the chest of Adi was a heart that almost forgot to beat, stricken to the core with a grief he had never known. Foundations now circled his heart, ready for walls to come rising. Had they risen too much, he would not now remember what he overheard someone saying at the funeral. It was his mother's brother "…she was just around at my place for a cup of coffee and sugar two hours before…" Penitence rung in Adi's distant uncle's voice as he said this to Dorian. Dorian was there too for a reason long forgotten. "When I find those bastards…"

The door opened with a sucking sound and awoke Adi from his daydream. The sensation was akin to that of being smacked across the face. Sudden. Talal sat across from him, fidgeting his fingers in a lock. It suddenly dawned on Adi, before Talal could talk, the last time he felt like his parents' little robin was at the funeral, where his childhood went down into the ground with her. And him. They were buried beside each other. Weren't they? Adi saw them, in their coffins, go down into the dark hole wet from rain the night before. He died. His dad was dead too. And part of who he was sat in front of him, back from the underworld, in flesh and bones. Haunting his being.

"Son…"

Chapter 25
By Astrid D'Coutho

Co-authors: Srikant Singhvi, Avani Painter, Aakanksha Deb, Malvika Dasani, Chaya Gupta

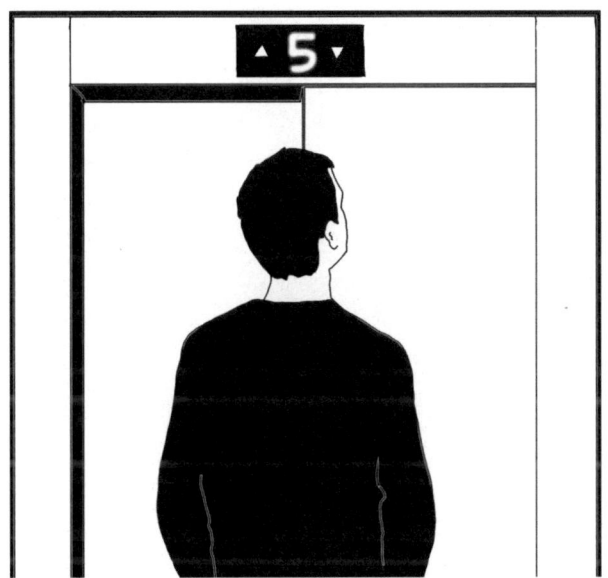

Illustrated by Lennita D'Coutho

Rob stumbled through the glass roller doors and into the lobby of his apartment complex. The security guard, an elderly gentleman who had seen Rob stumble in various states of intoxication many times before, didn't even twitch as he observed him, through narrowed eyes over the top of his newspaper, shambling through the elevator doors with blood down the front of his hospital gown, "Bloody addicts…spreading Seeker around. Keeping us in lockdown. Inconsiderate degenerate." He contemplated calling the cops but it wasn't worth the extra work at only 11.5 Mattas an hour. He returned to his paper with a smart shake of the sheets. The grumbling continued as the elevator doors shut and Rob slumped back against the back wall, trying not to pass out from exertion and nerves.

He reached the fifth floor and stumbled out, meandering down the hall toward his apartment door almost tripping on a bag of trash left near the garbage chute that had been sealed shut for maintenance. The sign was new.

He fretted silently about what he saw Ken do to those people back in Adi's lab. *He had turned them into monsters.* Their eyes dark and large were burning a hole in his head. He stumbled through the apartment door, not even registering that it wasn't locked and waded through piles of clothing mixed with old wrappers to the bathroom. Was Tara here?

Using the sink to brace himself, he looked in the mirror and saw a jagged splinter of wood the size of his thumb sticking out of his cheek. Rob's face and neck suddenly began throbbing with pain at the sight of his injuries and he yanked the splinter out of his cheek.

"AHHH!!" he let out a wolf-like howl that reverberated down his long hallway. He cursed Ken with every fiber of his being while simultaneously so very grateful that he had made it out of there alive. He had to get help to save Nadia. *Where was Tara?*

Suddenly he heard the front door open and close and the sound of fast-approaching footsteps. Before he could get himself to finish uttering Tara's name, two men in black jumpsuits and balaclavas burst through the bathroom door and advanced toward Rob. In his weakened state, Rob could only put up a faint struggle as the thugs held him down and smothered him with a rag. The way they easily maneuvered him to the ground and went about restraining him suddenly made them appear more than just mere thugs. They were professionals. A sickly-sweet aroma, like vodka mixed with sugar syrup, filled his nostrils as he faintly yelled for help before his vision faded to black.

Rob awoke several hours later sprawled on a couch in what appeared to be a moderately well-appointed green room. Gentle white lights shone down from the ceiling. His wounds had been dressed, his bloody garments had been removed and a new set of clothes was folded neatly on a side table along with a glass of water. As he attempted to prop himself up on his elbows, head throbbing, and swimming from the chloroform, he tried piecing together what fresh hell was about to rear its ugly head. He felt faint and exhausted and every muscle ached in demand for rest. He scanned the room again for a clue as to where he was.

"Look who's finally awake!"

Rob's head swiveled around to the back of the couch and his heart jumped out of his chest. He fell off the couch in a tangle of blankets and tried to find the source of the disembodied voice in the dimly lit room. Rob desperately looked around the room for the voice and his eyes settled on the blinking light of a camera that was recording him from the corner ceiling above the door. Rob grabbed at the sheets suddenly conscious of his exposed body.

The voice called out again…seemingly from the camera speaker, "Don't worry Rob, my name is Dorian and you're safe here. Someone will be down shortly to brief you on the current situation."

Chapter 26
By Gayan Ferdinand

Co-author: Onareen Ferdinand

Illustrated by Arman Iqbal

I was bleeding, wasn't I? Bloody hell. What have I gotten myself into now? I mean – thank you to whoever patched me up but, but – gosh I could do with a drink right now…

Rob heard a clink, as the door to the room was opened and left ajar, allowing a glimmer of a bright light to pierce through the darkness of the poorly lit room. A blinded, dumbfounded Rob exclaimed shakily, "Who's there? Dorian?"

But there was no response.

Rob picked himself up off the floor, and stumbled toward the door which was suddenly slammed shut firmly, with a bang. A red beacon light immediately illuminated on the ceiling, accompanied by a deafening siren on the lone-speaker in the corner of room, echoing all-around, forcing Rob to cover his ears and plead agonizingly, "Please, please stop! What do you want from me? Gratitude. You've got it. I'll do anything. Just – stoooooop!!!"

A split-second later, the blaring siren was silenced and the red light turned off, in unison. "Rob, you certainly are a funny guy. I promise you'll get out of here if you just follow my instructions. And hey, you're most welcome," replied a cocky, self-satisfied voice.

Gosh. There must be a way out of this room – This really doesn't feel right. Okay. Calm down, Rob. You've got this. If anyone does – you do.

"D-D-Dorian? Erm – yes. I'll do what you ask, just please tell me what's going on," stuttered Rob whilst frantically attempting to survey every inch of the room, still lying on the floor inches from the door.

"I knew you'd co-operate. Good choice. First thing's first? You'll have to get off the floor and get back onto your feet, because you'll need to do some walking. You'll be escorted to a special room where I'll tell you all you need to know. Capisce?" replied Dorian, in a friendly yet seemingly mocking tone.

After a couple of unsuccessful attempts to hoist himself up, Rob managed to crawl toward the door, using the door handle as support to eventually get to his feet. As he opened the door he noticed there was no trace of any light as there had been a little while earlier, but an eerie never-ending darkness, which appeared to stretch infinitely, was what greeted a wobbly, battered Rob.

"Off to see Dorian, are you?" bellowed a deep voice from a dark, imposing figure of a man that emerged from the darkness. "Just walk ahead of me," added the mysterious guide, who goaded Rob effortlessly through a series of hallways, lit by the odd emergency light which hopelessly attempted to illuminate their path. *A bit like my situation right now, eh? Bleak!* thought Rob.

The giant escort came to a halt and reached out toward a stainless-steel door with an access card, which resulted in the door sliding open to reveal a room – with four individuals in hazmat suits standing in a line, unwavering.

"Rob, nice to meet you. I'm Dorian. Have a seat," gestured to a man in a red hazmat suit, toward a chair with worn-out leather leg-straps and arm-straps. The cushioning was pilfered with holes, and the protruding discolored foam covered in stains of crimson.

"I'm not sitting in that! No way. What kind of chair is that!?" retorted Rob, aghast at what lay before him. In an attempt to make a dash for the door, his wobbly legs gave way. Semi-conscious, he awoke to see himself firmly attached to that ominous chair, with a spotlight fixated on his face. Dorian and three other individuals in hazmat suits surrounded him.

"Rob, there's no need to be afraid. You see, I know your friends – Tara, Nadia, and Adi," chirped Dorian, as Rob stared back blankly, but relieved at the mention of his friends. "You know them?"

"I most certainly do. You do know about Budlyt-19? My team of scientists here – have advised me that you got it. We tested you once you got here," continued Dorian.

"Wh-whaaaaat? No, no no no. I'm sure you've got the wrong person," stammered Rob as he looked to his right to see one of the hazmat suit-clad scientists walk a couple of steps toward him, and direct an infra-red heat gun toward his hand. "39.5'C, sir. Fever has risen since his arrival."

Gosh, I'm burning up? I can barely walk – but that's for another reason altogether. Damned virus. Did Ken get me?

"So, you see. You've been infected. But fear not, we're here to help you. In fact, Adi and Tara are eager to see you through this," said Dorian who appeared to be lost in thought as he made a summoning gesture with his right hand, resulting in a door being unbolted at the far end of the room. "ROBBBBBB!!!!!"

Is that Tara and Adi?!

"ROBBBBB – We've missed you! You've looked better but hey, you're still good!" exclaimed Tara in a slightly muffled voice through her respirator, as she crouched over to hug him tight.

"Let's go home and play some Street Fight IV, eh?" grinned Adi, as he too leaned in to hug Rob. *Was he on our side now? Was he always on our side?* So many questions.

"Guys, I've missed you so much. But this is a bit cheesy, and everyone's watching. Ease up on the love, huh?"

remarked Rob. Almost instantly, the dark room didn't feel so lonely anymore.

"Shush. Hugging with a hazmat suit is the new norm," laughed Tara. "I can still feel the love!"

"Sorry to cut in, guys – but he doesn't have much time," cut in Dorian. "Rob needs the cure – and you know pretty well who has it," as he pulled Tara and Adi away from Rob with a not-so-subtle hint of urgency.

Adi and Tara exchanged worried yet knowing glances at each other before Adi slowly moved forward and knelt by Rob. He reached out his hand and locked eyes with Rob, and whispered, "It's time to make things right. We have to save you and we have to start by saving Nadia."

Chapter 27
By Lennora Crilov

Co-authors: Darshil Shah, Reema Bhesania, Akash Chander, Shekhar Adnani, Venkatesh Narayanan

Illustrated by Channon D'Souza

Helicopter blades sliced the air as Charlotte, a group of decorated military officials and one of the greasy bejeweled men who was in the boardroom with her, raced toward LifaLabs to see how Ken was doing with Subject N.

As they neared the lab, Charlotte went over her plans again. After discussing the particulars of the transfer of an obscene amount of money to a Switch bank account of her choice and a lengthy discussion from the good Dr. Rosenberg on the various methods of administration of Seeker Cure as well as the weaponizing of the virus itself, Nadia, the magic goose, was going to be packed off to some hot and sandy ramshackle lab in the desert country of Thessi where she'd be made to lay golden eggs until she's a living husk of a human.

She barely flinched at the thought of sending a young girl away to her death and instead continued to muse over thoughts of swimming in precious caviar cream and that private chalet built into the face of the granite cliffs overlooking the river she saw on holiday once. She'd definitely be getting that. What better way to show the world who she was than by literally living on the edge? Free.

Charlotte lit another long menthol cigarette and continued to blow smoke into the faces of her companions, unfazed by objective coughs and the barely concealed look of irritation from the pilot. She puffed her way through four more till they could spot their drop-off location quickly approaching.

The helicopter descended toward the top of the building and two of the officers leaped out to assist the pilot in maneuvering and another to help Charlotte off, followed by the other passengers. The flimsy ladder swung in the powerful wind force from the helicopter but Charlotte descended gracefully, hair blowing dramatically, as if these moments were a commonality in her life. They walked down the stairwell and came out onto the floor where the labs were located and walked toward the door. The doorbell elicited a discreet chime inside the apartment.

As they waited, Charlotte noticed the door was brand new. Ken answered the door and the group hurried inside.

"We've had a problem…one of the patients escaped. I believe the subject to be infected but—"

An incensed Charlotte cut Ken off, "I thought I told you no more fowl ups?! It doesn't matter. Tell me you at least have Subject N under control."

"She's been sedated and ready for our first demonstration, Miss Yoss," Ken said.

Charlotte looked at him disgustingly, "The very first?!"

"The escaped patient, he um, caused delays…Adi isn't responding. Dr Rosenburg insisted on one healthy subject—"

Charlotte stared at Ken in disbelief, "Honestly, you men!" she spat under her breath. "You're like dolphins, not as smart as you're given credit for, only meant to be enjoyed on holiday and not to be put in charge of anything beyond jumping through a bloody hoop!"

She backhanded Ken across the jaw, her diamond cocktail ring leaving bloody scratches on his face. She leaned in and hissed, "This better work, Ken. Or you'll never be seen or heard from again. Where is Dr Rosenburg?!" she almost all but yelled.

At the sound of her name, Dr Rosenburg appeared around the corner, clipboard in hand, clipped expression in place. "A word, Ms. Yoss?"

Ms. Yoss probably had more than a couple of words for Dr. Rose, thought Ken because just a few moments later, quite similar to the beginning of a play, Charlotte, the bejeweled President of Thessi, and a few military men in ridiculous shades were seated outside the makeshift testing room, setting the scene for the performance that lay ahead.

Dr. Rosenburg took a step ahead and began to explain what they were about to see while Ken hung around the entrance itching to bring in the new and improved Melissa and Samuel. As the doctor rambled on about the subjects' initial reactions to the enhanced doses, which then progressed to a more stable state, Ken played with the keys to the room that held them. He could feel adrenaline coursing through him. He felt powerful to be a part of this moment. To play God.

"... as you will soon see. Ken?"

Showtime.

A few moments of shuffling later, two silhouettes appeared behind the glass. "Ready?" ventured the doctor but nothing could have prepared them for what they were about to witness. As Ken flipped the light switch, Ms. Yoss audibly gasped while the President sprung forward and clapped like a little child witnessing their first magic trick. Even the military men shuffled uneasily in the background.

Samuel and Melissa. Only they weren't. The thin green and purple veins that used to decorate their hands were now black and angry and seemed to be throbbing.

Their muscles have muscles, thought the President.

Dr Rosenburg passed around pictures of Samuel and Melissa taken when they were first admitted to the lab. The room was abuzz.

Ms. Yoss leaned over and whispered something in his diamond studded ear and his grin expanded to give the illusion it could at any moment split his face in half. He was one happy customer.

"And her?" he pointed one pudgy finger in Nadia's direction. She was already strapped into the bed against the wall, so unassuming you could have almost forgotten about her. But there she was; their most precious commodity.

Dr Rosenburg stepped ahead again, "Now that we know how to magnify the Seeker, we have to make sure we can neutralize it. Initial results show Subject N is quite possibly the cure. Given certain setbacks, we have had to delay our final test, but within the next 24 hours, we should know if we have the only cure in the world right here in Matana."

As Dr. Rosenburg and her mousy little assistant entered the room, Melissa and Samuel began to display some aggression but the metal shackles around their legs and a warning taser right by their necks kept them in check. Ken set off a few sparks every now and then for showmanship.

They were about to make history, right here in this room. Their names would be repeated in classrooms long after they were gone, every person on the planet would know their names.

Where the hell is Adi? How is he missing this?

Dr. Rosenburg held her palm out to her assistant who placed a long syringe in her hand. "Let us begin."

Chapter 28
By Lennita D'Coutho

Co-authors: Yash Yadav, Sakshi Agarwal, Abigail D'Coutho, Hannah D'Coutho, Ambika Luthra

Illustrated by Nishant Mishra

Ken paced about the lab gathering equipment and placing it into boxes. The delicate beakers clanged in time with his thoughts. Time was of the essence. Now that Nadia had been auctioned off like a prize pig to the highest bidder it was time to make tracks. He allowed his mind to play with the possibilities his future carried while his hands kept busy.

Just as he was shuffling around, his phone started buzzing in his back pocket. He idly reached for it expecting it to be the procurement team but was puzzled by the absence of caller ID.

Who could it be, Ken wondered to himself. He answered the call and a voice breathed into the phone saying, "Ken, it's me, Adi... I'm on an untraceable line, don't hang up!"

Ken went blank for a minute, then started yelling over the phone, "ADI?! Where the hell have you been, it's a shit storm over here, dude! Where did you go after that chick Tara escaped? The higher-ups have been breathing down my neck wondering if our department has been compromised because of your screw up! Get your ass back here now, we've secured a buyer and need to begin moving the subject N to the next location! Oh, and the weird kid you brought it got away too."

Weird kid?! Rob shot daggers at the phone – *coming from the creepiest dude he ever met?* He replayed the moment his foot connected with Ken's face to assuage his temper.

"Calm down, Ken, the situation with Tara is still ongoing, and forget about Rob, he's not a threat... I was taken hostage. Cryptop found me." Adi started weaving the excuse of the century as to why he suddenly dropped off the map.

He continued over the phone to Ken, who had gone silent, "Tara had set a trap for me. I saw her posting on social media and found her location..." here is where he began to lie so as not to give away Talal's location, "she made it easy to find her by going right back to her apartment and in my eagerness to retrieve her I didn't consider she had done so deliberately…"

Ken was silently taking all this in as he continued rushing around, not fully believing what he was hearing. He couldn't believe Adi had been captured by Talal's group of hackers and somehow escaped, unless he was compromised, he mused.

"…and I didn't consider Talal's goons would be waiting in ambush, I'm still not sure how they found Tara so quickly. After a bullshit lie detector test and interrogation that barely cracked me open, they think I've defected over to their side. I'm using this opportunity to bring Tara in when she's vulnerable but I've not found the right moment yet."

Ken was full of doubt, but at this point Adi and even Tara were superfluous to the overall plan. He decided to throw Adi a bone.

"Look Adi, take care of Tara, kill her if you have to but do it quickly, I can't cover for you for too much longer, Subject N will be moved in 24 hours now that payment has gone through and we know she and the others are stable. Luckily it seems Tara's either extremely dumb or too scared because we have seen nothing on her account for some time now. Get back here and get back on track ASAP!"

He bought it, he freaking bought it, Adi thought to himself, relieved. He needed to figure out what Nadia's movements were going to be in the next two days if they were to save her.

"What do you mean subject N? Nadia?"

"That girl is our golden goose, Adi, she is the cure! She's already been auctioned off to the President of Thessi for a butt ton of moulah!"

Adi was thinking on his toes at this point, now that he knew who the buyer was he could figure out a way to put him off the deal. He also needed to take control of the time window somehow to make sure he knew when Nadia would be moved.

"If Tara is no longer a priority, I'll assist with moving subject N. What's the drop location?" Adi was praying that Ken would let slip where the Thessi President was waiting for Nadia to be handed to him. That way he could figure out both how to get to him and how to intercept Nadia. He had never been this nervous before. He was full of adrenaline as he waited for Ken to respond.

"We are moving her tomorrow night, from the apartment complex to the Matana Casino Hotel. The president will be there in the Presidential suite along with his retinue to make the exchange. Then they'll take subject N to the airport via helicopter and we'll go buy some cars!" Ken chuckled sickly as he casually discussed human trafficking. "Anyway, stop mucking around and I'll see you at the labs tomorrow night. Be there on time, I'm sick of covering for you." Ken hung up and Adi nearly swooned as he regarded his own luck.

Adi took a second to catch his breath, he looked up from the phone, staring at Talal who had been listening in with Tara and Rob and a few other operatives and nodded.

Talal looked up at him and said, "Game time, boys and girls. We need to scare the president off this deal somehow. He has been accused of aiding and abetting in trafficking before but this leverage might be enough to scare him off."

Talal motioned to his team, "Start combing surveillance footage around the apartment lab, the deal most likely went on there, any phone, microchip, speaker, whatever! Find usable proof of the deed and we've got him, we just need to figure out how to intercept Nadia."

Tara and Rob both looked around the room, hoping blindly that this near impossible plan could save their friend. Adi looked at them and said, "We'll get her back, guys, you'd be surprised what finds its way into some form of recording… I'm still linked up to the labs' security systems. If that deal took place near any form of lab tech, I'll be able to find it. Don't worry, we'll get her back." *We have to,* Adi thought to himself.

He observed the chaos around him; Talal was busy giving orders to an associate, Rob had a permanent look of worry on his face, Tara was scurrying around trying to be helpful, and Dorian had discreetly stepped out to take a phone call.

There was a shift in the room.

As they all thought about how to save Nadia, for the first time in a long time, they finally felt the world shift in their favor.

Chapter 29
By Heather Chung

Illustrated by Channon D'Souza

Adi hung his head in his shameful, sorrowful hands for the first time. Oh, how desperation makes you do the unthinkable. He sat out of place whilst everyone else conducted the rest of the plan on how to save Nadia successfully. They all knew it wasn't going to be an easy operation despite the glee, optimism, and hope they collectively shared. "Son?" Adi groaned, snapping his hands away to hide the tears. "What?!"

"Oh son, that is not a polite greeting."

"Well, I'm sorry for the lack of vivaciousness!"

Talal shuffled two meters next to Adi and was met with a desolate silence. Many questions and thoughts rushed back into Adi's head sitting next to his father. But none manifested. It's funny how sometimes anger can paralyze someone from wanting answers.

"Do you remember when you were young?"

"Jeez, what the hell is this?!"

"Nothing."

"I know what you're doing. Don't!"

"Can't I at least try?"

"Oh, so you're finally going to resume your fatherly duties now? Okay then." Adi turned to face his father. "What could you possibly want to tell me?"

"Don't be sarcastic."

"Oh, I'll be however I want!"

"Yeah, and look where that got you. Oh, right. Here! In this mess!" Talal pointed. Adi rolled his eyes before sitting back square to view the huddle. Talal sighed...before standing up and leaving Adi to his tortured mindset. *Insolent old man!*

Rob peeked at this supposedly tender moment that you see in films, only to be disappointed that there was no father-son embrace but rather footsteps walking toward even more hurt and turmoil that may never get fixed, even under a crisis like this. Rob hobbled over to Adi... Even with a slightly fuzzy head and questionable friendship/enemy status of him and Adi, Rob had to know more about what was to become of Nadia. "Rob, seriously don't! I know!"

"Hey! You don't need me to tell you how messed up this all is…"

"So, what? Is this the part where you tell me that I am still a good person? That I am redeemable? That I can truly fix my wrong doing?"

"I think that can only be done through actions at this stage."

"Rob… Mate. I'm sorry… I…"

Rob interrupted by holding up his hand. "Adi, that's not enough. Because right now, Nadia is in danger. Shouldn't it hurt for you to know that?" Adi nodded. It was worth a try at least. "Adi… Can I just ask why? Why did you feel the need to do this? Why would you put her in danger like this?"

Adi shook his head and remained quiet.

Maybe the guilt was settling in. He didn't want to admit that he wanted the fame and fortune like *everyone* does. He wanted to be known as part of the team that cured Budlyt-19. Everyone loves an underdog story and he wanted to be the star of one. He wasn't going to let anything happen to Nadia, but…

"Fine, don't answer." Rob turned around. "Just make up for it by getting Nadia back. It's the least you can do." He huffed and hurried back to the table where everyone was gathered.

Adi gazed forward, ignoring their presence to view the dark clouds covering over the sunsetting blue sky…

"Nadia? Come on!"

"Adi. No!"

"Please! I want to show you something!"

The lab stood with brightness and promise for better things to come. This was the moment when Adi first got a job at LifaLabs. "Are you even allowed to give me a tour? I'm not staff."

"No, but you're family!"

"Well yeah, but I didn't get the job. Ergo you deserve the perks."

"Would you just...please!" She nodded and accepted Adi's hand to drag her around. They ended up in a glass tunnel, looking down at the hard workers with pipettes and color liquids. "I can't believe this. I'm really proud of you, Adi! You get to be on the frontline of where there's going to be research and cures to SO many illnesses! Do you reckon you'll be able to help with what you have studied?"

"Paha! Don't make me laugh! I only got the job as an assistant. I'm responsible for cleaning out beakers, test tubes, work spaces, and insane amounts of paperwork."

"Yeah so? You show them your big academic brain and work hard like you have been doing. Who knows?!"

"Hey don't be mothering me now."

"You know what I mean, Adi!" She elbowed. "And besides, what's wrong with throwing you a compliment anyway? We all need to do it more often. So, take it and shut up. I'm really proud of you!" She lifted her arm and side hugged him. Both smiling at the new environment and life that Adi had worked so hard for.

Adi shook his head to snap back into focus. He finally stood up and approached the table, with as much authority and stiff upper lip attitude as possible. "We need to go... NOW!"

Chapter 30
By Elisabeth Ten Cate

Illustrated by Lennita D'Coutho

Panic bloomed in Ken's gut. When he had blurted out that they would be moving Nadia the next day, he had felt as though he had bought himself ample time to assess the strangeness of the situation. Yet time seemed to tick quickly now. He had feigned casualness whilst name dropping a mixture of facts and fiction. He had also sounded appropriately irritated to convince the people on the other side of the line that he was blind to their deceit. The Adi he knew would never ask about the project in such a careless manner.

The capabilities of Cryptop, he knew, should under no circumstances be underestimated. The group of hackers, clouded in mystery, was notorious. Anyone involved in the dealings of LifaLabs knew to be wary of Talal, Dorian, and their accomplices. But if they had managed to recruit Tara so shortly after her escape, they must have been aware of what was going on for far longer. *Had they infiltrated their systems ages ago, or had there been a traitor in their midst?*

Drowned in thoughts he walked over to the only computer present in the lab. *They would surely try to break into our systems,* he thought as he logged in. An easy job, given they had Adi. Changing his password would create suspicion. They would instantly know that he had not been fooled by the call. Yet if he could continue his act of oblivious naivety, there was a chance he could climb a rung in LifaLabs' hierarchy. Changing the password was not the way to go, so he made a copy then wiped the camera recordings of the past two days from the mainframe and replaced them with a duplicate of the recordings of the two days prior to that. A black hard-disk now kept the only records of what had transpired, which he slipped into a discreet flap inside his jacket.

Friend or foe, he thought as browsed through the company's employer database. Adi's face revealed as little in the photograph as it did in real life. Charming, controlled, and always vigilant. At least, until he had made the error of allowing Nadia into the apartment. As she had entered their domain, impulsivity had penetrated Adi's otherwise composed demeanor. Even so he had remained in charge, on the receiving end of the boss' messages and giving orders. Ken had not met, or in fact been aware of, Ms. Yoss until very recently. If it had been Adi that betrayed them, he had delivered a stellar act.

Could it be Dr. Rosenberg? he wondered. Was it possible she had entered their lab in disguise? Her eternal frown stared at him from the screen. What would be in it for her though? Her entire education had been funded by LifaLabs, so a betrayal of this magnitude would seem unusual.

Ken's face now moved one profile down. The fiery red locks of his controversial ex-colleague stood out. He remembered the day Aaron Keen had been dismissed after catching the virus. He recalled the commotion his death had caused in Matana's media. His liquidation in such a public spot had been an error of judgement. It had been necessary, Adi had said, withholding an explanation as to why. Like everyone they had looked at the detailed pictures that had emerged in the papers and it had unleashed an inexplicable fury in Adi. "Bloody rat," he had shouted. Ken had not understood why, but as he pulled up the images from his gruesome shots on the news, his eye fell on a detail he had overlooked last time around. The contours of a key designed with the makings of a motherboard were visible on Aaron's wrist. He had been the one and they had found out too late.

As adrenaline rushed through his body, his phone rang. He took a deep breath before answering because he did not want to come across like an uncontrolled child in front of his superior. Ms. Yoss sounded neutral. "I want you to double check we have at least ten percent of our stock left before we travel," she ordered without delay. "Once you have done the count, I want you to add it to the log." He was unable to respond.

"An 'of course, Ms. Yoss' or an 'at once, Ms. Yoss' would be in order," she reminded him.

"I'm sorry, Ms. Yoss," Ken answered dutifully. "I'm really sorry, but I have discovered something serious. We have been betrayed and Adi's been intercepted by Cryptop."

What seemed like the longest seconds he had ever lived passed in silence. But then Ms. Yoss' voice sounded again. This time he could hear her think as she articulated each word.

"Yes, I know," she said. "It's all part of the plan."

Chapter 31
By Mildred Sharma

Co-authors: Hazel Carvalho, Cheryl Soares, Jason Pinto, Bindhu Pradeep, Doreen Mendez

Illustrated by Arman Iqbal

"It is time to settle things," Charlotte said to herself. She had been in the shadows for too long and it was time to come out. The wheels of justice were moving too slowly and Ken was the grease that would see things along. He had come to uncover more than what was required, but she knew that already. His admission made no difference.

She crossed her legs and watched Ken spin around Adi's apartment looking for proof of Adi's betrayal. She watched in amusement for a few minutes more, then spoke, "Sit, Ken. There's no real need for more information, anyway I think that first we should clear the air; specifically the fact that his whereabouts have been unknown to you for much longer than you've been letting on." She stared at him with an icy countenance that somehow made Ken want to melt into the floor.

How could she know? He had been so careful in his attempts to conceal Adi's absence. Was this all a part of her plan?

As he pondered this thought to himself, Charlotte continued, ignoring his apparent concern. She reached inside her Hermur alligator bag and pulled out photos of Adi bent over a desk with another man, both looking engrossed in the papers and plans that had been laid out. "Anything familiar?"

Ken stared down at the grainy picture that appeared to have been taken from security footage then stared back at her.

She continued, "That's Adi with one of the main overseers of Cryptop. His name is Talal. Do you recognize this man?"

Ken remained silent and shifted uncomfortably in his seat. He did not like how this situation was unfolding and he felt beads of sweat form on his forehead.

"How long did you think you could go without being found out, Ken? How long were you planning on keeping it a secret that you lost not only Adi, but two other test subjects,

Tara and Rob?" Charlotte's icy eyes were fixated on Ken now, like a frog locking onto a fly.

"It wasn't my fault, Miss Yoss! He was not thinking clearly and I had no control over what he did, he just left!" Ken spat. "He called me on a secure line telling me that he was on our side! He's trying to infiltrate Cryptop and steal secrets for us and bring the subjects back! And regarding the security, Ms. Yoss, I—"

Charlotte continued, seemingly unconcerned by Ken's protests, "Not only have you lost a key operative who has had access to our systems and secrets, you have also unwittingly given him cause to turn against us. You see, years ago I was the one who orchestrated Adi's parents' attempted murder via a car crash. Only I didn't count on his father surviving. I also did not count on his father joining Cryptop and becoming my fiercest opposition."

Ken stared dumbly at Charlotte, "F-father?! Adi never said anything about his father! And, what do I have to do with—"

"Yes, that's because he believed his parents are dead!" Charlotte was on her feet, pacing now, her icy resolve had melted giving way to trickles of anger turning into rivulets. "Now he has discovered that Talal is in fact his long-lost parent, the father he never had…all thanks to LifaLabs."

Ken stood there bewildered at her wild rant. It was as though her temper had very little to do with him but more with herself.

Charlotte took another breath and felt her phone vibrate in her hand. She glanced at the screen and walked toward her bag then began pawing through it, "I couldn't get rid of him like I got rid of the others. His connections run far and wide and his disappearance would raise too many questions. Luckily, I preemptively set up my own intelligence source in Cryptop so I could keep an eye on things. He was stubborn at the beginning, but," she smiled, "everyone has their price, everyone has their value. Yours just ran out." She pulled out a small pistol and shot Ken in the chest at point blank range, splattering blood all over white couches.

As Ken lay in a rapidly expanding pool of blood, her phone was still vibrating incessantly in her hand matching the thump of adrenaline in her heart. "Hey, I was just wrapping up some loose ends. Are we still on track?"

Charlotte smiled at the response she received as she wiped blood off her heel and began her way out of Adi's apartment. "I know, I can't believe it. We're so close!"

Before she reached the apartment door, she took a deep breath to appreciate and revel in the moment. *Finally.* "I can't wait to see you. Love you too, Dorian. I'll call you when we reach Matana Towers."

Chapter 32
By Nishant Mishra

Co-authors: Dushyant Mehrotra, Risha Gill, Shamveel Mohammed, Reem Mohammed Muneer, Akshat Mishra

Illustrated by Nishant Mishra

Blood. The vehicle of stardust that feeds the human machine.

For Ken, people were just bodies to be experimented upon. He believed science was independent of emotion and he felt his detachment was what made him a good scientist.

He felt his mind involuntary dissolving in between hazy memories and sharp painful reality...charged for murder and organ theft for black market sale back home, his escape to Matana to disappear and find his next score.

He flashed back to the start of his time at LifaLabs and how he wished to add a brick to the edifice of the human body. Stabbing pain brought him back to reality.

Ken was now laying in a pool of his own elixir on the floor, semi-conscious as it dripped from his ashen face. His head was reeling with pain from the wound the bullet had inflicted. He was barely breathing as he heard Charlotte answer her phone, "…can't wait to see you at Matana Tower. Love you too, Dorian."

Ken tried to focus and piece together what he heard. *It seems that that glacier of a woman was in it for herself all along,* he thought to himself. *I don't think so.*

Ken did a quick assessment and inspected the bullet hole, finding air bubbles at the opening, his lung was slowly collapsing.

Adi. He needed to call Adi now. It was the only way to bring down Charlotte. He groaned as he reached into his pocket and pulled out his phone, blood spraying the floor as he coughed and fumbled as he pressed the call button next to Adi's contact number. The phone began to ring.

Meanwhile, at Cryptop headquarters Adi and Talal were poring over the logistics of a possible rescue plan. They needed to find audio or video compromising enough to scare the President away without a fight. Dorian and Tara were skimming security footage they had found of the airport as well as the perimeter of LifaLabs' base of operations and Rob was listening intently to various recordings being gathered from bugged enemy communication hubs. All to find Nadia and bring her home.

Adi let out a moan, "Not a single lead! Nothing to bargain with if we plan to intercept before she reaches the casino. If the exchange is made and if she gets to the airport, it's over!"

Tara turned around while Dorian remained fixated on the screens, "Adi, please, we're all trying our best. The worst thing would be to lose our heads…we will get her ba—"

"How can you say that?! We are hours away from losing Nadia! What do you just think the solution is going to fall into our laps?!"

Tara bit back her retort. *How could I say that?! How dare he!* She pressed her jaws tight together until they hurt.

"Adi!" Sensing the shift in mood Talal grilled from the other side of the table. "Your attitude toward your friends is appalling, we are doing our best!"

Tara looked over at Dorian, who had seemingly drifted off into some riviera of thought where he was far away from all the conflict unfolding around him. She even thought she saw him chuckle silently at Adi's and Talal's quips at each other.

Adi's anger masked his shame. *I'm such a hypocrite,* he thought. She was where she was because of him. Wasn't she? But like a wounded animal, he tried to bite back to fend off more pain, "What about that message you sent her that led her right to Lifalabs' doorstep anyway? If I didn't add her to the trial, she would have gone missing like everyone else!"

Suddenly, a marimba ringtone pierced the tension as Adi's phone started ringing. Kens name flashed across the screen. The room was dead silent except for the jaunty song that kept madly repeating.

"Adi, pick it up, he could help us!" Tara motioned toward the phone. "We might be able to weasel some more details out of him. It's worth a shot, we just keep hitting dead ends! He might be able to give us the evidence we need to twist the President's arm!"

Dorian spun around in his chair and addressed Talal, "That would not be advised. Do you not think it curious that Ken is attempting to make a call now? This has *trap* written all over it!"

"Dorian, what's gotten into you? We need to try everything we can right now," Talal said.

"I must protest!" Dorian was on his feet now, hands balled into fists. He was shaking. "We already know where Nadia is. Why not simply knock out all the power and take her by stealth? They'll never know what hit them, especially if we entrust this with my personal team of operatives." Dorian was getting desperate.

How is he still alive?! he thought to himself.

The phone stopped ringing. The room was quiet for a moment, then the marimba tone started playing. Ken was calling again. Without taking a moment to think Adi slid his thumb across the screen and accepted the call on speaker. The whole room went quiet, waiting for a sound from the other end of the line.

Then a voice rasped over the phone, sounding as if the speaker was gargling a mouthful of tar. Coughing and more rasping and then, "…Adi?! Adi, listen to me! I don't have time. I'm out of time. It's over for me, dude, I messed up…trusted wrong people…"

Ken was rasping and gargling more now. Adi spoke, "Ken, what are you—"

"Adi, there's no time. We've all been played, man. There were never gonna be any cars! No damn golden eggs! Listen to me! Nadia's location was a lie. She's in Matana Tower where Yoss lives. Her location was changed."

More wheezing, "There's a back hard-disk with information you might need."

Adi went silent, trying to fathom why Ken was suddenly being so accommodating with information. Ken kept talking, "She shot me, man! She freaking shot me!" The pain in his voice made everyone shift uncomfortably around the room.

"Who shot you?!" Adi was completely out of his depth now.

"MOLE! Yoss has a mole in Cryptop! He's been reporting to her since the beginning! She's orchestrating some sort of sleight of hand crap where she and this guy she's playing house with take the money and run!"

The room was silent, Adi and the rest of the group were completely flabbergasted. A mole. Their worst fears had been realized.

Ken was wheezing now, he could barely speak, "Do it for your dad. She can't get away with what she did."

Adi muttered, "Ken, man…I, I don't know—"

Ken cut him off, "It's Dor-Dorian."

Adi stared at the phone as Ken started coughing more, the wet sounds of blood pooling in his lungs punctuating ragged breathing and then, silence. The phone disconnected.

Dorian stared around in disbelief, his long braid almost as bushy as the tail of a cornered cat. He made a dash for the door in a desperate attempt to escape.

TWACK! Dorian found himself on the floor in a tangled mess, head bloody and unconscious, Rob holding one of his crutches over his head like some strange mallet.

Everyone started at Rob and Dorian. The air in the room was still.

"Never liked his pretentious vocabulary anyway," Tara said.

Chapter 33
By Azeen Gorgin

Co-authors: Mahmoud Fahmi, MarieAnne Al Shami, Wafaa Al Shamsi, Dijana Al Bayati

Illustrated by Channon D'Souza

Nadia awoke dazed. Her head felt heavy due to the sedatives that had been forced into her and her senses were submerged and muted. She was no longer in the lab, she knew that much. She tried to recall anything that could make sense of the situation she now found herself in. Eyes closed in an attempt to settle the spinning in her head, she felt around with outstretched hands at her surroundings.

She noted that she was lying on top of soft sheets and satiny pillows and a pale orange glow through her eyelids from the lamps on either side of her bed, the soft breeze from a ceiling fan kept the room at a comfortable climate. Aside from the humming from the fan, there was silence. She was alone.

It was a welcomed change from the cold, sterile room she had been confined to that reeked of disinfectant and from the incessant hum of the fluorescent lights that were kept on day and night and the humiliation of being kept in a backless paper gown that creep Ken would peek through as he administered to her against her will what he called his 'cocktails.'

Nadia shivered at the thought of not knowing what was inside her, coursing through her veins and changing and affecting her body and not being able to refuse or cry out. She felt dirty and violated. Her body felt foreign.

She opened her eyes and sat up slowly, looking around what she now saw was an opulently outfitted kind of guest room. She looked at the foot of a bed and there she saw a change of clothes and a gold embossed card propped up on top of them.

Nadia pushed off the heavy embroidered blankets and clumsily made her way to the bottom of the bed. She retrieved the card, which she saw was embossed with an intertwining "CY" sitting on a green chiffon dress and pieces of jewelry and a set of green heels neatly laid out for her.

"There is a guard outside your door. He will bring you to me once you are presentable. Try anything and you'll be shot in the kneecaps and dragged here. Remember, you are always being watched."

Nadia clasped her hand over her mouth to stifle a sob. She began to cry in dismay and wonder at how her cousin could have betrayed her like this. How could Adi have thrown her into the lion's den and left her for dead?

She remembered Rob and how he had promised he'd save her, he said he had a plan. She scoffed at the thought, *Rob has a plan, yeah right,* she thought to herself. She mused about Rob and how he never really had much of a plan at all. Ever. Always hanging around doing nothing. Nadia caught herself. Her experiences made her feel cynical and jaded. Even if she managed to get out of this alive – then what? Would she ever go back to being the carefree girl that loved being around people? Would she ever be able to trust another soul again?

Suddenly a loud banging came from the door, then what Nadia could only presume was the guard's voice called out, "Hurry up! You don't want to keep the boss waiting!"

Nadia jumped, startled out of her thoughts and back to the present. She shakily got out of bed and began dressing. She stepped out of the room and was walked down the hallway by a large suited man with no neck, toward large ceiling-high doors that had been left ajar, firelight flickering through onto the surrounding walls and mirrors.

She stepped into a large well-decorated room where she saw a tall blonde woman standing at a stone work desk wearing a deep blue gown with diamond earrings. She looked up from her work as Nadia walked in and scoffed, "Couldn't you have at least run a comb through your hair? You look a mess. Your buyer will be here any minute now and here you are looking like a pig in a wig. That dress is couture, try doing it justice."

As Charlotte eyed her through narrow slits, she couldn't help but pause for a moment on Nadia's arched brows and sharp cheekbones. *She is quite beautiful,* she thought. *Pity.*

Nadia stood there silently, not knowing what to say to the woman's comment. Then she began slowly walking forward toward the desk. She knew this person was attempting to keep her off balance so she quickly fired back. "Pig in a wig though I may be, still valuable enough to have a buyer, as you put it. Isn't that why you threatened to shoot me in the knees and not the face?"

Charlotte lifted her own perfectly shaped brows at Nadia. *Ohhhh, beautiful and brave.* Nadia was met with laughter from the other side of the table, "Oh look at you! Proud that the meat on your bones is worth more because it's sweeter, you're still going to get eaten, little girl. And your little friends have forgotten all about you too!"

Nadia's lower lip began to quiver, but she kept talking. Talking would buy her some time to think of some way to escape from this place.

"My friends will find me! They've probably already contacted the authorities and told them—"

"Told them what exactly, Nadia?" The woman started walking around the desk toward her. Her cold icy blue eyes locked with Nadia's as she continued, "Only your cousin and your friends know where you were taken, albeit vaguely. With all the confusion of maintaining strict lockdown, the Matana police department has enough on their plate and won't be bothered with the business of a missing girl, especially since no one will be telling them, especially not your friends Tara and Rob."

"They're my friends! What makes you think they won't do everything in their power to find me and take you to jail!?" Nadia was desperately looking for an exit, a weapon, a phone, anything! She didn't know how much longer she could stall her captor.

"Because your cousin, Adi, made short work of them after they broke out of the lab, their bodies are now being processed into raw materials for other lab trials. I know it's too bad, but Adi is quite excited about buying his new Ferrari with his cut of the money… I hope that in light of your cousin's betrayal, it gives you comfort knowing that they struggled till the very end."

The woman grinned sardonically, watching horror overcome Nadia. Nadia slowly sank into a nearby chair and trembled. Her friends were gone, Adi had betrayed her, she had been abandoned and not even her family knew where she was. Just as sudden as she felt her heart clench, she felt the pain subside and a sudden feeling of resignation ebb throughout her body. This was her life now. She had to give up and accept it.

Suddenly there was a commotion outside the doors and cries and then the sound of breaking glass and pottery. A guard burst into the room, with blood pouring from a gash in his head, then collapsed onto the rug. Behind him were two figures in hazmat suits.

They stepped into the light, and Nadia gasped, there standing next to each other, were Rob and Adi, who said, "Hey cousin, don't worry, you're safe now."

Chapter 34
By Paige Ng

Co-authors: Rohit Samuel, Sacha Daswani, Aliya Shetty, Yanet Kidane, Salim Shaw

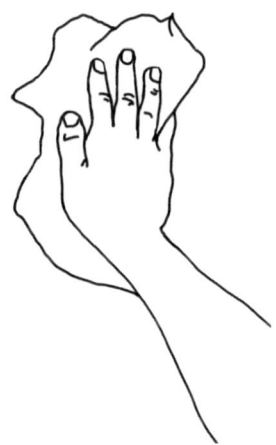

Illustrated by Lennita D'Coutho

A large bump in the road caused the car to shake, violently juggling around all of its passengers. Nadia was being sped away yet again, but this time she was safe. The fight to win her freedom had been quicker than she thought possible.

"It was easy," Adi pointed out, "we honestly just pushed through the doors. We found this service entrance for the building at the back and we were able to bypass security and cameras to get to you. Dorian's intel in the building helped a lot." He thought of that scumbag tied up at Cryptop headquarters, blue-faced and scared.

"I'm never letting you go again!" Tara clung to Nadia as if she was at risk of being lost again. "I was so freaking scared, Nadia."

"So was I…" Nadia locked eyes with Adi in the rear-view mirror and shot an accusatory glance his way. She was still unsure about all of this but anything was better than being sold like cattle to further a maniac's desire for world destruction.

Adi looked away guiltily, unable to look her in the eyes once since they had been reunited. He attempted to move the conversation along to avoid any confrontation, "Anyway, we need to stop by the apartment lab to retrieve some equipment and tools needed to synthesize a cure from Nadia's blood, then we can help Rob."

Her eyes turned to settle on Talal. *Uncle Talal.* She could hardly believe it. He caught her looking and shot her a smile that took her back to her childhood. He promised to explain everything to her later. Right now, their limited time had to be put to better use.

As the car pulled up in front of the building where the lab was, Nadia shivered at the idea of going back to that place. But right now all she could think about was Rob and how vulnerable she felt without him. She felt tired and exhausted; all she wanted to do was forget this whole ordeal had ever happened. She slipped her hand into his as they made their way inside. He squeezed her hand back assuringly.

As they walked through the hallway toward the lab, Nadia saw flashes of the horrors she had been subjected to: being forcibly sedated, abused, and subjected to Ken's vile presence. Though she was immune to the virus, she still felt tainted because of him. Talal and two Cryptop agents entered the lab before they did to do a sweep, Adi and Nadia waited anxiously outside for the all clear.

"We found a body!" yelled one of the agents. Another couple of agents had been sweeping Adi's old apartment as well for signs of Charlotte. They had found Ken's body now bloated and purple in a pool of his own dried blood. Talal whistled and looked in Adi and Nadia's direction and remarked dryly, "You can see why I wasn't keen to have her stick around, temper!"

Adi bent down to recover the black hard drive Ken told him about. "Is it wise that we let her escape? What if she comes back for Nadia?" Adi asked Talal.

Talal replied, "Cornering a woman like Charlotte is dangerous, like cornering a wild animal. She poses no threat now that she's lost Nadia and her capital which was all tied up in priceless black market artefacts that are all over her house. She's nothing without her image. She'll be back, but not for a long time."

Charlotte had screamed and yelled as they rescued Nadia, but no one paid any attention to her, except for one brief moment in which Talal stared her down and calmly recounted how Dorian was finally outed and was now at their mercy. Never had he felt the urge to hit a woman, but that vile snake was hardly human. She was a murderer and had destroyed his family. It took every ounce of strength to leave her with a heavy warning to never be seen in this city again.

Adi and Nadia entered the lab and she was immediately filled with a sick feeling, she swooned noticeably and Adi reached out to help. Nadia involuntarily shrank away, before straightening up and wordlessly following Talal and leaving Adi in her wake with a look of self-pity on his face. He sighed and followed suit.

"Right, accessing the data needed to blackmail the president of Tessi into leaving without a fight will be much easier now that I have a copy of all the original footage right here. This won't take long. You two, go to the equipment room and gather up equipment for a blood transfusion. Rob is stable but the sooner we get you guys on the road the sooner he can be relieved of his pain."

Adi and Nadia silently picked through the supply closet for the list of equipment and tools necessary for extracting Nadia's antibodies. Time seemed to drag on as they mindlessly gathered medical supplies. Nadia couldn't bear it any longer, "Why did you do this to me?"

Adi turned to Nadia with a hopeless look in his tear-filled eyes, "I've been broken for a long time, Nadia, ever since I lost Mom and Dad. I have felt empty and adrift. I wanted to create a legacy of my own and I got carried away—" Nadia put her hand up to stop him.

"So you offer me up as cannon fodder? Your own cousin? How could you, all for money?! I don't think we can ever come back from this Adi, you have lost me. I don't know how to bring myself to look at you anymore, I just see fear."

Tara hung around protectively and stepped in to help. She knew Nadia needed answers, but she couldn't take seeing her friend so weak and upset. She motioned to Nadia to hand over the equipment.

In the background Talal walked off to instruct the team to wipe all prints and remove all traces of their presence in the apartment and coordinate a police informant in their employ to guide the authorities to Ken's body and to get their stories straight.

Talal motioned for Adi to come closer, "The police will be here and I'd rather none of you be here to complicate the issue. The commissioner and I are professionally acquainted and will very enthusiastically accept any testimony to avoid making me an unhappy chappy."

Talal looked at Adi's drawn features and then at Nadia, "Give her time, what she's been through will take its toll and she needs to work it out herself." He hugged Adi close, "And with you."

As they pulled away from the building, their team sped away toward Cryptop headquarters, Adi kept staring at Nadia's face illuminated by the flash of police lights and sirens and wondered if they would ever be whole again.

Chapter 35
By Devika Sharma

Illustrated by Nishant Mishra

6 Years Later

Nearing sunset, a fire alarm could be heard ringing from a posh suburban two-story, framed by powerful, tall red oaks. The loud wailing carried down 22nd Surabhi St. causing two men in checkered vests to peer curiously in the direction of the noise. Quickly deciding that this slight inconvenience shouldn't have to deter him from making his standing 6 pm tee off, Vishnu, the residential community advisor, walked straight to the boot of his shiny new SUV, flung his golf bag in, and quickly drove off, friend in tow.

Relieved to see the rear lights of her neighbor's car disappearing over the curve of the road, for the second time that week Nadia found herself running for a broom to poke at the noisy device to shut it up. It was only Tuesday.

As she thumped at the ceiling, three young children came bursting through the kitchen door, hoping with abandon to witness another one of their mother's glorious kitchen fires. Depending on which invested party you asked, there was both fortunately and unfortunately the absence of one.

"Lennora. Lennita. Shouldn't you be upstairs helping your brother get ready? Everyone will be over soon," Nadia said as she placed the burnt oil in the steel pot under cool running water, causing a magnificent sizzle to escape from the sink.

The littlest, a rosy-cheeked boy of three, clapped.

Nadia felt a smile tugging at her cheek as she reached down to scoop him up.

"Mister, is this chocolate on your face?"

With playful admonishment, she turned toward the twins, "Girls, I made it very clear that no snacks were to be had before dinner."

Lennora, whose hands were still behind her back, slowly presented her mother with a colorful drawing of one of her latest favorite cartoons. "Look, Ma! I got an A! Miss Daisy said I'm the best in class, better than Becca, even!"

Lennita interjected, "No, she didn't, she said you both got the highest—"

"Anyway, Mommy, could I get a new crayon set? There's a new one called Cal's Colors that Becca's been using and—"

"Girls, mommy has to get dinner ready, okay? Be good and help Matt. I've kept your clothes on the bed, please go get dressed. Later, we can discuss the crayons."

Lennora burst into a wide smile that made Nadia's heart warm like the oil. Burn, even. Her twins were growing up so fast and with their dark hair, dark eyes, and olive skin, they were like looking into a mirror at a fun house. Her, but smaller.

Matt, who was nearing 3, waved goodbye and walked out of the kitchen with his sisters, hand in hand. With his feathered sandy blond hair, playful smile, and easy blue eyes, Nadia would often comment that Matt would never feel left out around his siblings, because he had a soul twin of his own: his father.

A bitter smell shattered her loving reverie. *Shit! The pie!*

Switching between a curse and a prayer, Nadia opened the oven, and unthinkingly reached to pull out the apple pie without mittens. "MOTHERF—"

"Darling? Are you okay?"

Ignoring her husband, Nadia ran to the sink and shoved her fingers under the tap, half expecting a cloud of smoke to rise from the reddening skin. Her fingers were smarting.

He walked around the black marble kitchen island toward the dining table, pulled out a chair, and placed it under her.

"Sit," he commanded.

Nadia gratefully motioned toward him with puckered lips, planted a soft kiss on his lips stained from pocket mints, and proceeded to recall the events of the day. He burst into peals of laughter. Slouched over, his hand clenching at his stomach, he managed to utter, "Should we just order from Kunal's Kitchen? We can get the stir fry you like."

"I guess," Nadia conceded, surveying the mess around the kitchen. She instinctively cringed at the thought of cleaning up so allowed her eyes to linger over his navy suit, open white shirt, and relaxed tie instead.

"You, my love, are brilliant in every way, but cooking isn't really your thing, leave that to your cousin," he said as he picked up his phone that began to ring.

"Hello, Rob speaking. Hi, Nishant, yes sorry, I just got home. I'll have to send you the documents tomorrow, I'm a bit tied up right now," he smiled as Nadia slid his tie up into place.

"Yes, everything looks great. We're as excited to get ink on the paper and start moving on Gayan Gaming," he paused to allow his potential new investor to rattle on, "perfect, talk tomorrow,"

Nadia silently giggled while Rob hung up, rolling his eyes, "Man, that guy can talk."

"So it's finally happening, huh. Good news all around tonight! Come here, I'm so proud of you!" Nadia flung her arms around his shoulder. He had come such a long way. "Wait till it's signed, then we celebrate," Rob replied, picking up his briefcase, loosening his tie once again, shooting her another questioning look that was met with, "I'm fine, I'll put this away and ring KK's." Satisfied, he headed upstairs to greet his kids.

Given the absence of a father figure in his own life had made him worry about what kind of father he would be to kids of his own. Turns out, he was pretty good. Sure, they each had him wrapped around their little finger, he was the parent they would ask for that extra scoop of ice cream late at night, he would stay up playing video games with them, and buy them extra toys over the holidays, but he was stern when he needed to be, and he was fair. God, he didn't think his life would turn out this way. They blessed his life when he needed it the most. They needed it the most. They breathed life into their collapsing existences and helped them create new memories so bright and beautiful that they made the old, bad ones retreat into distant shadows.

His youngest was standing in the doorway to his sisters' room, gaping. Rob walked quickly inside to find his two little angels in the middle of a fist fight. "Girls! What are you doing? Lennora, get off her!"

"Oh, hi, Daddy," Lennora replied, climbing to her feet.

The casualness in her voice in stark contrast to the yelling and thrashing rendered Rob temporarily discombobulated, "Uh, hi, are you going to tell me what happened?"

Lennita, whose hair resembled a bird's nest flung from a tornado, responded with, "Nothing, Daddy. Sorry, we will get ready now," and proceeded to take her clothes from her bed to the bathroom. Lennora followed suit.

A week ago, Rob was testing out a new game, Rakesh's Revenge, to launch under his gaming company, and against Nadia's judgement, allowed the highly impressionable 5 and 3-year-olds to sit around in oversized bean bags with oversized popcorn buckets to watch. He suspected that the main character who liked to run around town yanking people by their collar claiming, "Snitches get stitches," had something to do with their new-found moral code and shook his head in amazement. He was so focused on graphics and programming, he had completely overlooked how many colorful one-liners the girls soaked up over those 8 hours. He even helped Lennita work on her pronunciation of 'snitches'.

Shit. Nadia was not going to be happy with Rakesh at all.

He looked at Matt who was playing with a fire truck and seemed to have forgotten the whole ordeal already.

"'Sup, little buddy, you good?" said Rob, making a mental note to have a conversation with the girls before Nadia caught wind of any of this. He stepped into the master bedroom and heard the doorbell ring. He glanced at his watch; it was only 7. No one was expected for another hour.

He walked over to the barrister and caught Nadia making her way across the living room to the main door. A melodious greeting floated in. "Mrs Mira!"

He ducked even though she couldn't see him and ran back into his room and shut the door. He shot Nadia a text saying *Good luck* before jumping into the shower.

Downstairs, Nadia felt her phone buzz. She sneaked a peek and stifled a laugh as Mira's ample bosom bounced around almost knocking her phone out of her hand.

"You really should be more careful, dear! Had I been home, I would have rushed over to make sure everything was fine. But I had a meeting with the school board, then with the new NIKI charity association, I did tell you I was also appointed as a board member with them, didn't I, and some last-minute shopping. It's been absolutely exhausting!" she exclaimed with an exaggerated sigh.

"Anyway, Avish sent me a message from the golf course, something about a fire alarm but a super important game with Vishnu, and I came as soon as I could, dear," she went on.

"Just one of those days in the kitchen," Nadia responded with a watery smile.

Not one to shy away from fluorescents even in her late sixties, she reminded Nadia of a giant bumblebee with her curly brown poof and yellow shift dress, complete with yellow stones along the hem.

"Quite right, dear," her voice dripping thick like honey. "OH, is this new?" Mrs Mira sauntered in, uninvited, and stopped in front of a giant painting that hung over the fireplace to assess the painting Nadia had completed a few days ago. It was a sensory awakening watercolor of her childhood home. Even if one had never been there, she imagined that they too could smell the freshly cut grass, feel the crisp, clean air, and see every inch of candy clouds swirling under a star-studded sky, just as she remembered.

"It is, I just fini—"

"Is it for sale? I know a few ladies from the club who would just DIE to own something like this. Leanne, she has quite the eye, that one. She would snag this up right away, dear! Or, maybe for Elisabeth's new summer home. What's this going to cost?" Mrs Mira asked, tapping her garish heel on the floor.

"I wasn't planning on—"

"Actually, let me get them to call you. Let's get a bidding war started! Then lunch with mimosas once I'm back in town! Celebrate the sale! Oh, I do love a mimosa! Should one choose to have one with her breakfast in place of a coffee it might be regarded as day drinking, but on your account dear, it's a celebration!" she cackled at her own joke, wrapping her pink color talons around Nadia's arm.

"Anyway dear, gotta run, Azeen said she would be here after meeting with her obstetrician for your dinner cum watch party? Adi on the news! How marvelous. I must insist we all meet once I'm back in town, give him my love," Mrs Mira said, tottering around the paver insets and natural stones along the driveway.

Relieved, Nadia closed the door behind her and went to fetch the last of the garbage bags to dispose of before her guests arrived.

At 8:15 pm arrived the first of the guests, Nadia's school friends turned art world curators, Samad and Julia, carrying a lush bouquet of blue and white Hydrangeas, and a bottle of wine.

"Soraya. It's this delicious pinot I tried the other weekend. You're going to love it," said Samad, "and from the looks of it, you need it. What's up? You okay? You look tired," he observed.

"She has three kids, Sam, of course she's tired," Julia quipped.

Nadia got her friends some glasses and her only victory from the kitchen, a charcuterie board loaded with delectable meats, cheeses, artisan breads, olives, and fruits, and they made their way into the cozy living room, fireplace ablaze.

As they caught up over some work chat which then moved to work gossip, as it usually does, Rob entered smelling of soap and aftershave and offered to refill their glasses.

The doorbell rang again.

"That must be Jeremy, I'll go get it," he said.

Julia sat up a bit straighter and fixed her hair. She used the surface of her phone screen to check her makeup.

Noticing, Samad nudged Nadia, causing them to giggle like they would back in high school when they would find out their friends had a little crush.

"Shut up," said Julia, phone still in hand, criticizing her appearance.

As Jeremy entered, Julia swiftly swiped her thumb to unlock the phone, making her appear very much as if she was in the midst of reading an incredibly important email or an article about environmental degradation, as opposed to indulging in frivolous vanity checks a split second ago.

Everyone hugged, inquired about each other's family and health, and another bottle of wine made its way to the table. A collection of soft rock started playing on the speakers.

Another ring.

A tiny human came running in through the room, past the adults who were busy preparing the table for dinner, and went upstairs.

"Paige! What did we say about running? Please behave!"

A beautiful woman in her last trimester entered the room immediately stirring a cocktail of admiration and jealousy amongst other women in the room who had either endured a pregnancy of their own or one day wished to, as Azeen was one of those genetically blessed few who managed to contain their pregnancy weight to just their belly. Everything else had magically remained tanned and toned.

"Hi, hello everyone! Sorry, we're late. Took forever at the obstetrician and then we caught some traffic on the way back," she paused to sit down, graceful even with limited balance and motor function.

How she could be born a product of Mrs Mira...

"But I see we made it right in time for dinner, lovely, what are we having?" her husband, Benjamin, continued.

They really were a stunning couple right out of the pages of a glossy lifestyle magazine. On first acquaintance, the information that both of them worked as successful human rights lawyers was always immensely impressive yet slightly disenchanting.

A chime rang out through an upbeat drum solo.

Food or Tara?

As she approached the door she could hear Tara's contagious laugh on the other side. Her best friend was finally here. She missed her and needed to see her. Especially today...

"Hiiiii!" Tara wrapped her arms around Nadia, engulfing her in a cloud of her perfume.

"Vanilla bean and... I want to say cinnamon?"

"Very good! What do you think? Got it last night," said Tara.

Her life as a talk show host presented her with the luxury of shifting through the newest products sent straight to her doorstep.

Standing next to Tara was a man Nadia did not recognize.

"Nadia, this is Dinete. Dinete, Nadia."

They exchanged hellos and Nadia ushered them inside.

"Cute," mouthed Nadia.

"For now," Tara mouthed back.

Tara was so busy with her rocketing career that she did not have time for dating. And from what Nadia gathered, she was quite happy to keep it that way. The men that accompanied her, much like her perfumes, changed each time they met.

"There's our little celebrity!" exclaimed Samad. "Sit right next to me, I want to know everything about Azmeen! I caught the interview last week, tell me, what's she like in real life? Give us all the dirty details."

"Sorry?" said Azeen.

Samad and Tara laughed.

"A-z-M-e-e-n!"

"Oooh, yes! I meant to catch the rerun. Nadia! Julia! Come over here, Tara's about to tell us about the Azmeen interview."

The ladies and Samad gathered around the hardwood edged red sofa, while the rest of the men stood a little away near the fireplace holding their whiskey in hand blown glasses that were gifts from Nadia and Rob's wedding.

They appeared to be deep in conversation about a game they caught last night, but every man, ever so slightly, tilted their head to pick up snippets about the sexy singer.

"Diva. Wanted sparkling water chilled to 6° C at any given time, sunflower seeds with shells, three dedicated limousines, yellow in room lighting, dedicated butler, and absolutely no request for autographs or pictures to be made by any of the staff," responded Nadia to her friends who were leaning in close, lapping up each salivating detail.

"Her music has been sitting at the top of the charts for over 12 weeks so… Go figure," Tara continued, "Zaha on the other hand was a real sweetheart; incredibly down to earth. To be handling all that fame and working in the movie industry at only 16, it must be treacherous, but she has a great team behind her."

The group nodded and murmured about fallen young talent lost to pretentiousness and corruption.

"Who's up next?" asked Julia.

"Actually, my boss, Mildred, is in conversation with a VIP businesswoman who is meant to be making a big comeback to the city. She's working on securing an exclusive interview with her in a few days. It's all very hush hush, until it has all been finalized, no one – not even me – knows who Mildred is in conversation with," Tara paused to take a sip of her wine, "but whoever she is, I can't wait. I'm looking forward to speaking to someone who isn't missing a few buttons on their remote control."

Nadia snickered and put her hand on Tara's shoulder, giving it a gentle squeeze.

She addressed the room, "Guys, Rebecca and Astrid said they won't be making it in time for dinner. They're running late at the lab and they're probably going to catch the interview over there with the rest of the team. Should we eat?"

25 minutes later, after polishing a spread of duck, orange chicken, spicy vegetable stir-fry, and dumplings, and putting the kids to bed, Nadia and her guests sat around a large 4K 75-inch screen to watch Talal and Adi's television interview. It was being broadcasted by Matana's highly coveted news channel, Matana by the Hour, at primetime. The excitement was palpable.

"If only Adi was a woman," Tara mused, "I could have had him on my show instead."

A few years ago, when it became trendy to call oneself a feminist, Tara was just starting out as a host and quickly moved to making her talk show a platform to only celebrate strong and successful women. It was a bold idea that worked. Tara felt her first pang of regret since.

"This is so cool!" said Julia and Samad who were huddled under a fluffy pink throw blanket.

"It's starting!" The identifiable station theme song with red and blue flashes across the screen alerted them that the segment was about to begin.

As the camera cut to frame Adi, Talal, and the city's beloved anchor couple, Aleena and Osman, Nadia's living room erupted into applause.

The song ended on a crescendo and after a brief pause, Osman began in a deep baritone, "Good evening, Matana. Thank you for joining us today in welcoming two of our city's finest minds, and here to tell us more about one of the most revolutionary advancements in science is Mr. Talal and Mr. Adi from Heather Corp. Welcome, thank you so much for being here."

"Thank you so much for having us," Adi responded. He looked so handsome. The years had added a spattering of grays, making his facial lines more pronounced and though his expression seemed weathered, he had an air of distinction about him that shone through his eyes.

Talal shifted proudly next to him, "It's great to be here."

"Welcome! So for our audience back home, could you tell us more about Heather Corp and the miracle 'cure all' your team has been working on?" Aleena said, immaculately dressed in a neat white suit, not a hair out of place.

"My father and I founded Heather Corp, named after my mother, 5 years ago," said Adi motioning toward Talal, "after the Budlyt-19 pandemic. He has always had exceptional vision and philanthropic ideologies and his revolutionary thinking that has lead us to develop a cure that is potent, ethical, and most importantly, universally accessible."

Smiling, Talal responded, "My son likes to downplay his involvement, but he runs the show."

There were a scatter of *awwwws* around Nadia. As she continued to watch, she felt rows of goosebumps erupt over her skin. She was so proud.

The night after Nadia was rescued, she locked herself in a hotel apartment for days. He waited outside the whole time until she was ready to talk. But it would be years before she could forget what he had done. Forgive what he did. But he was there every day, apologizing, fixing, mending, absorbing the abuses, the hate, the rage, waiting patiently for Nadia to feel like was willing and able to finally move on. He was the best uncle to her kids and their relationship was as strong as it ever was.

"Tell us about Edenseed," said Osman.

Adi cleared his throat, "In my youth, my parents had already conducted a decade worth of research surrounding the fabrication of a kind of broad-spectrum viral cure capable of unzipping and neutralizing the offending virus's DNA. Edenseed is smart, and is constantly learning. So far she is capable of managing and curing over 130 different dangerous viruses."

"That's incredible," claimed Aleena, "so how far are we from approval for mass production and general use?"

"We're getting there. Of course, we want to make sure she is thoroughly and exhaustively tested, first. In the meantime, there is the matter of funding. We are in conversation with a few investors, but we want to make certain that the people we bring on board are properly aligned with the long-term goals and future of the company."

More claps. The wine was really flowing now. Nadia caught Rob's eye from across the room and they shared a smile. They did it. All of their suffering was not for nothing.

Azeen tapped her, "Hey, what's up with Adi?"

Nadia quickly looked back at the TV; Adi seemed to have frozen in time. His demeanor shifted as he teared his eyes away from his phone that he clumsily pushed back into his pocket, unclipped his mic, excused himself, and without waiting for the hosts to respond, he disappeared out of frame.

Talal asked him as he walked past if everything was okay but Adi did not seem to hear.

After a few uncomfortable seconds, Talal joked about a possible problem at the lab, and the interview resumed. It lasted for another 15 minutes. Adi never returned.

"I think I should call him," said Nadia as she stepped into the kitchen, Tara followed her.

"Must be a work thing like Talal said, I'm sure everything's fine," soothed Tara, reading the look of worry all over Nadia's face. Rob came over to listen to the call. It went straight to voicemail.

"He's on another call," said Nadia.

"I'll try Talal," said Rob.

After a few more attempts, Rob returned with the news that Talal wasn't answering.

Samad and Julia, who joined them in the kitchen, were filled in on Adi's and Talal's strange behavior. Everyone assured Nadia that there would be a perfectly normal explanation and to not jump to conclusions. No amount of wine nor support from her friends could palliate the nervous beating in her chest. Nadia couldn't shake the feeling that something was very wrong.

"Oh, in the meantime, here's a fun distraction," said Tara, "my PA said our next guest has been confirmed. She'll be sending me her bio and prep questions shortly. Wonder who this bigshot magnate could be."

Nadia rested her head in her hands, trying to remain calm, surely she was overreacting and she didn't want to ruin the evening. She watched her phone on the glass table. *Ring*, she willed it, *ring!* What was it they said about watched phones? That they never...

Nadia's phone lit up and began to vibrate on the table. Adi! She grabbed it, stabbing at the 'answer' button.

"Adi," she exclaimed, "is everything okay?"

He didn't immediately respond. When he did he sounded like a man who had lost everything.

"Nadia, I'm so sorry. She threatened the kids. She wants to come back to Matana."

"Adi, who—" Nadia paused, then felt a hole open up in the pit of her stomach as realization came over her.

"She wants to come on board as VP of Edenseed; says she will tell the world what happened with LifaLabs, what I did to you... After Dorian got life in prison and she was banished, she has nothing to lose. She knows where we all live, Nadia. She said she would hurt the kids," his voice cracked.

Tara was oblivious to the on goings between Nadia and Adi as she checked her email. She found the email marked 'GUEST BIO AND QUESTIONS.'

She downloaded the attachment and waited for the file to load. The loading circle on her phone was replaced by the open file. Tara's throat chocked as the blood ran cold in her veins.

There's no way. There is no way this is happening.

The woman in the photo staring right back with piercing blue eyes was Charlotte Yoss with the title 'VP of Heather Corp' underneath.